Tell Me, Bella

TELL ME, BELLA

A selection of stories by
VAHAN TOTOVENTS

Compiled and translated
from the Armenian by
MISCHA KUDIAN

MASHTOTS PRESS · LONDON
1972

Foreword and English translation
© Mischa Kudian 1972

Published by
MASHTOTS PRESS
BCM-Mashtots
London WC1

ISBN 0 903039 01 X

Made and printed in Gt. Britain by
Ebenezer Baylis & Son Ltd
The Trinity Press
Worcester, and London

Contents

Foreword

VAHAN TOTOVENTS, one of the leading Armenian writers of this century, was born in 1893, in Western Armenia, in the small country town of Mezré, about 150 miles to the south of the Black Sea port of Trebizond. He was one of seven children, and he was only eight when he lost his father—a prosperous landowner and a high government official. After an elementary education, the young Totovents went to the Armenian Central School in the large nearby town of Kharpert, where two of his teachers were well-known authors, who influenced his style of writing, despite its individuality. His first book appeared in 1908. The following year he went to America, where he worked as a salesman in a store. At the same time, he mastered English and French, and studied literature, history, and philosophy at the University of Wisconsin.

During the First World War, in 1915, Totovents went to the Caucasus as a volunteer in defence of his country: this was the year in which the whole of Western Armenia was depleted of its Armenian population during the notorious Turkish massacres and deportations. He was actively engaged in the efforts to relieve the untold misery, famine, and epidemics, brought about by refugees fleeing across the border into Eastern Armenia. He edited a newspaper in Tiflis in 1917–18, wrote numerous articles, a novel, literary studies and other material. In 1920 he again went to America, and two years later he returned to Eastern Armenia, by this time known as Soviet Armenia, where he devoted all his time to writing. His output comprised novels, short stories, plays, and poems.

His most famous work, *Life on the Old Roman Road*, was written and first published in 1930. Its English translation, published in London in 1962 under the title *Scenes from an Armenian Childhood*, was an outstanding literary success. It deals with the author's reminiscences of life in Western Armenia in the 'nineties, with its colourful background.

Totovents had intended writing a long novel about the blood-stained and heroic history of the Armenian people with their miraculous resurgence from the ashes of the Black Year of 1915 into a prospering state, but he did not live to achieve this aim, due to his untimely death in 1937, at the age of forty-four. He did, however, write a faceted sketch on this theme, here entitled 'Tell Me, Bella', in which the narrator and his companion, Setrak, return to Armenia from America as volunteers and upon revisiting the latter's home town find it deserted except for the handful who had fled to the mountains and caves during the massacres. This story reflects something of the background of the life and events during the period of Armenian history in the first quarter of this century, as do the remaining stories in the present volume: hence the title of the book.

M. K.

Pale-blue Flowers

THERE WERE BARELY a few people at her funeral: her sister, Tourvanda Korro; Tourvanda Korro's husband, Krikor-the-Saddler; her husband's brother, Simon; two neighbours with their wives; the priest and the beadle—the priest had arranged for the clerk not to come, so that the money they would receive would be divided between two, instead of three. Her husband had lain in the cemetery for a year and had been waiting for her.

They buried Sara beside her husband.

Before they left the cemetery, the priest demanded his reward, and once outside the fence, they all separated.

Krikor-the-Saddler said to his wife:

'Well, wife, I had better go to the shop.'

At the house of mourning, the only person waiting for Tourvanda Korro was the orphaned five-year-old Torrig.

When earlier, with tearful eyes, her black shawl over her head, and one hand on the coffin, Tourvanda Korro was leaving the house, she remembered Torrig. She left the coffin, went inside, opened the cupboard, took a piece of dry bread, gave it to the boy, sat him on the mattress, and said:

'Sit here, my little pet. I will be back soon.'

Torrig took the bread and began to gnaw at it.

Tourvanda Korro caught up with the coffin.

And when she returned from the funeral, Torrig had nibbled away half the bread; with the remaining half he was playing a game with the kitten. The kitten gambolled about, nipped the piece of bread, while the boy tugged at it, freed it, and laughed.

Seeing that Torrig was totally unaware of the misfortune of being deprived of the most precious person on earth, Tourvanda Korro's heart sank again. The plaintive weeping at the burial arose once more in the blackened, miserable, tiny, and tottering cottage.

There was no one, absolutely no one in the whole world apart from Tourvanda Korro to look after the orphan. So that, without any decisions to be made, she picked up Torrig, wrapped him up in her black shawl, and took him to her own house. There she lit the fire immediately, heated some water, bathed the orphan, and put him to bed to sleep. Then she washed his clothes, spread them out in the scorching sun, dried and mended them; when the orphan woke up, she dressed him and waited for her husband's return.

In the evening, when Krikor-the-Saddler came home, Tourvanda Korro took the orphaned infant in her arms, stood before her husband, and said:

' "There should be a kid in the house," you used to say. Well, here's one: you can pretend that it has dropped from my loins.'

Tourvanda Korro and Krikor-the-Saddler had been married for twenty years, but in spite of their fervent efforts—they had lit countless candles in front of pictures of saints—they had not produced any children.

Krikor-the-Saddler looked lengthily at Torrig, who was smiling away with a foolish air. He took pity on the child and, releasing a tolerant smile from behind his moustache, took him from his wife's arms, kissed him, and said:

'God has turned His eyes upon us again.'

'What would have happened to him, if it wasn't for us?'

'He would have been thrown among the street urchins in the ash-mounds of the bath-house,' replied Krikor-the-Saddler.

Tourvanda Korro once more cried for her poor, unfortunate sister, who was already resting in the cemetery, and upon whom was spread the deep shadow of the mulberry tree.

Both Tourvanda Korro and Krikor-the-Saddler developed a deep love for Torrig. They both felt anew the tragedy of having no children of their own; but barely a few months had gone by when it seemed to them that he was born and bred in their house. As for Torrig, he was an amazing child: he would neither cry nor would he get into mischief; he would stay wherever they put him down; he would wake up in the morning in the position they had laid him to sleep the night before; if they gave him food, he would eat it, if they did not, he would not ask for it.

'Torrig, lad,' would cry out Krikor-the-Saddler when he returned home from the shop, 'how are you?'

Torrig would turn his head round calmly, he would gaze at Krikor-the-Saddler and smile vacantly.

'He is God's lamb,' Tourvanda Korro would say.

'He is a little like a cow,' Krikor-the-Saddler would disagree. She would glare at her husband angrily.

And Tourvanda Korro would sit Torrig on a mattress which she would spread on the floor and she would say to him:

'Torrig, my precious soul, I am going to the market to buy some things. You sit here on the mattress and play.'

Then Tourvanda Korro would shut the door and go to the market; and even if she did not return for hours, Torrig would not go beyond the limits of the mattress.

When Krikor-the-Saddler remarked one day:

'There is no fire in him at all!'

His wife replied:

'Don't talk like that! God has already dealt him a blow: he is an orphan!'

Krikor-the-Saddler remained silent, but he could never reconcile with the thought that a son of his own would not have been such a miserably stupid child. Without any good reason, he believed that if he had had a son, he would have been different: an exceedingly lively, bright, and clever boy.

No one knew what made him think so.

Krikor-the-Saddler often spoke with feeling about this subject. One day, Tourvanda Korro lost her patience and said angrily:

'You couldn't produce anything all these years. You became the father of a ready-made child, and now you don't like him!'

Krikor-the-Saddler became silent about this subject once and for all.

And Torrig grew up. He had big, strong bones, but his head remained relatively small.

'His head is very small,' remarked Krikor-the-Saddler one day, even though he had long decided not to say anything.

Tourvanda Korro did not leave him without response:

'Let it be small; what can we do about it? We are not going to crack nuts on his head!' she retorted.

'It would be better if it grew a little bigger, so that something could get inside it!' growled Krikor-the-Saddler.

Tourvanda Korro did not answer, but she glared at him in a peculiar way.

And it would happen that Krikor-the-Saddler would take Torrig out for walks. When Krikor became entangled in conversation with somebody in the street, Torrig would wrap his arms round the saddler's leg, and he would stand there quietly.

There would be no sign of impatience: he would stand there and wait until Krikor-the-Saddler had finished his talk—talks which often went on for a long time. Torrig would be so good on these occasions that it became a constant habit for Krikor-the-Saddler not to go anywhere without him.

'Let him stay at home,' Tourvanda Korro would say. 'He might be a nuisance to you.'

'No, wife, he is never a nuisance. He takes hold of my leg and just stands there. He is a very good lad.'

Tourvanda Korro would be filled with unbounded joy.

'The orphan has found a home, and we have got ourselves a child. If we had waited for Krikor-the-Saddler, nothing would have come of it,' she would say.

Gradually, both Krikor-the-Saddler and Tourvanda Korro felt that Torrig was an indispensable part of their home.

'What would we have done if there wasn't this lad?' Krikor-the-Saddler would ask.

'What would we have done? We would have sat and looked at one another's miserable face,' would reply Tourvanda Korro.

'Torrig, my lad,' would call Krikor-the-Saddler.

'Yes, Krikor Agha?' Torrig would answer promptly.

'Get me some water to drink.'

Torrig would fetch the water.

Tourvanda Korro's happiness would have no limit especially when Torrig would call her husband 'Krikor Agha'—this was something which she had herself taught him. If no one on earth was likely to address her husband by the title of 'Agha', at least, Torrig would do so.

'Torrig, my pet, who is knocking on the door?' Tourvanda Korro would inquire, knowing fully well that it was Krikor-the-Saddler.

'Krikor Agha,' would reply Torrig.

Tourvanda Korro would swell with pride and, delighted, she would take hold of Torrig's head, would press it to her bosom, would kiss him and say:

'May your Krikor Agha worship you!'

When Torrig grew older still, he became useful outside the house also. It would be:

'Torrig, lad, take this meat home!'

'Torrig, lad, take this bread home!'

'Torrig, my child, go and tell your Krikor Agha to get some vinegar, and bring it home!'

'Torrig, darling, take the basket to the shop!'

And Torrig would do everything without a murmur, without any complaint. Only it would take him a very long time to go from the house to the shop and back again. When Krikor-the-Saddler came home and found the meal not ready, he would be astonished:

'Haven't you got the meal ready yet, Tourvanda? I am starving, wife!'

'You sent the meat home late.'

'What do you mean? I sent it this morning!'

'But it was midday when Torrig came home!'

'Torrig, lad!'

Torrig would stand there and look at him obediently.

'Did you bring the meat straight home? Didn't you go anywhere else on the way?'

'No!'

Torrig was not lying: he had gone straight home from the shop, but he had loitered so much on the way. Everything in the street interested him: if he came across a bear-show, he would stop and watch it; if he saw chickens feeding in front of a house, he would stop and watch them for a long time; and if he happened to see two united dogs, he would watch them for hours, in wonderment and delight, without knowing what was taking place. Sometimes it would happen that as he watched, somebody would snatch some bread or vegetables from under his arm. He would be delayed most of all on those days when the snow came down in large flakes. The leisurely, fluttering, and dancing particles of snow would give Torrig immense pleasure. He would lift up his head and wait until a snow-flake landed on his eyelashes.

One day, while he was busy watching something, a dog snatched the meat away from his bag. He chased after it, but could not catch it. That evening Krikor-the-Saddler slapped him across the face and said:

'You must pull yourself together, my boy; that meat cost us money!'

Torrig cried.

'I won't do it again, Krikor Agha!' he sobbed.

Torrig uttered this in such a way, with such misery, with his head bowed, and in such a helpless tone, that Krikor-the-Saddler's conscience was stricken, his eyes became moist, he turned his face away, not to show his tears; but Tourvanda Korro could not contain herself and wept volubly together with Torrig.

'Why did you strike the poor orphan? May you break your hand!' said Tourvanda Korro.

That night, when they went to bed, Tourvanda Korro turned her back on Krikor-the-Saddler.

'Tourvanda dear, why have you turned your back on me?' asked the other, with surprise.

'Even that is too good!' replied Tourvanda Korro, annoyed.

'What's happened again? Is there a new moon?'

After a long silence, Krikor-the-Saddler managed to turn his wife's face towards him.

'You mustn't raise your hand against the orphan. What answer am I to give my sister on the other side?' she said.

'That was something that happened, wife. I won't do it again,' promised Krikor-the-Saddler.

A little later, he stroked Tourvanda Korro's face with his bushy moustache.

'I feel sleepy; keep to your side!'

And silence prevailed.

There was something which had greatly puzzled Krikor-the-Saddler and Tourvanda Korro: Torrig used to wear out his clothes in a place which should not normally have done so. No one else's did. This was the part of his sleeves from the shoulder down to the elbow, instead of just at the elbows.

'I will go mad!' Tourvanda Korro would exclaim. 'How does he do it?'

'I would understand it if he wore out the elbows, but why higher up, my dear?' would ask Krikor-the-Saddler.

One day he secretly followed Torrig to find out what he did.

And it all became clear.

Torrig rubbed against the walls all the way as he went: on one side from the shop to the house, and on the other from the house to the shop.

And one day, they hung a wooden writing-tablet on Torrig's chest and took him to Mister Ashour's school that he might learn to read and write.

'His flesh is yours and his bones are ours,' said Krikor-the-

Saddler, implying that the teacher might beat up the boy short of breaking his bones.

Mister Ashour looked at Torrig from under his spectacles: the boy stood there erect, with arms down and shoulders slightly raised.

'He looks intelligent,' said Mister Ashour.

Krikor-the-Saddler swelled with pride.

'He has taken in all that his eyes have seen, teacher,' he said.

Torrig went to Mister Ashour's school for three years and barely learnt the Armenian alphabet, but not at all how to read.

Tourvanda Korro stubbornly insisted that Torrig should continue his schooling.

'He hasn't got a head for lessons,' gently protested Krikor-the-Saddler.

'He'll learn one day,' countered Tourvanda Korro.

'If he can't read and write he must be an ass, and won't become somebody,' persisted Krikor-the-Saddler.

Tourvanda Korro laughed quietly and said:

'You can't read and write either, are you an ass also, eh?'

Krikor-the-Saddler kept quiet.

And Torrig continued his school until Mister Ashour himself sent an ultimatum saying that the boy had failed to change his class so many times that he was now with the little children and he could not keep him at school any longer.

'Do you remember, wife, how his father was also a bit of a numbskull?' said Krikor-the-Saddler.

'You don't bark at the dead!' reprimanded Tourvanda Korro.

In the end, Krikor-the-Saddler suggested:

'I'll take him to the shop: let him learn my trade and become somebody, like myself.'

This time Tourvanda Korro agreed, because the boy's upper lip was already turning dark, his voice had grown deeper, and it was positively plain that not only did he have no love for learning but no aptitude for it, either.

On the first day, Krikor-the-Saddler gave Torrig a long-winded advisory lecture in the shop:

'Torrig, my boy, no trade is big or small; every trade has its worth, because every trade saves people from being poor and in need of others; saddlery is a trade, a very good trade: now you ask me "Why?" '

'Why, Krikor Agha?'

'Because your business is not with men, but with donkeys. Why are you laughing, with all your teeth showing; because you heard the word "donkey"?' said Krikor-the-Saddler, hurt.

Torrig immediately became serious, but he wanted to say that he had heard a donkey braying; fearing a slap, however, he remained silent. Krikor-the-Saddler continued:

'Don't get it into your head that this is an easy trade. No, my boy, no, every trade has its tricks!'

'It has, Krikor Agha,' voiced Torrig mechanically.

'Uh-huh! That's what you've got to learn: the tricks!'

'I'll learn them, Krikor Agha; it's nothing.'

'Don't talk big like that; we'll see what you're made of!'

And Torrig started working.

To begin with, he managed to learn how to sew, how to stuff with straw, how to prepare string, and so on; but when it came to the difficult part, the external shaping of the saddle, he came to a standstill.

Serious discords developed between Krikor-the-Saddler and Torrig—so much so that the Saddler would shout at the boy in the shop, in the presence of others:

'You've got a donkey's head! I must make a saddle for you too! I have told you how to do it forty times and it hasn't sunk into your brain yet!'

'But a donkey doesn't know the difference, Krikor Agha!' Torrig would protest.

'Right, a donkey is an animal and doesn't know anything; is its master an animal also, boy?'

Sometimes the argument would grow so hot that Torrig would leave the shop, he would go home and say to Tourvanda Korro:

'Auntie Tourvan, Krikor Agha doesn't like me: I am not going to the shop any more.'

'Everybody learns a trade that way, child; he, too, has been banged on the head many times!'

Torrig, with head hanging down, would return to the shop.

'Uh-huh? Feeling less puffy now?' Krikor-the-Saddler would ask.

Without replying, Torrig would pick up the bodkin and begin to work.

Discords would occur also over sales. In the absence of Krikor-the-Saddler, Torrig would sell saddles at less than cost price.

'Why did you sell them so cheaply?' the Saddler would ask.

Torrig would look at the Saddler, with frozen eyes, and would not reply.

'Answer, you animal!'

'It was just something that happened; I won't do it again!'

'How many times is it you have done this now? You have become like a wood-worm to me, you son of a dog!'

On one of those days Torrig returned home drunk: something which had never occurred before.

'Oh my, what has happened now? This was all we needed!' cried out Tourvanda Korro, beating her knees.

But in the morning, stroking Torrig's head, she asked him why he had got drunk.

Torrig replied:

'It's better if I go and lie next to my father and mother.'

'Why?'

'Krikor Agha upsets me so much,' complained Torrig with tearful eyes.

Nevertheless, time wiped out everything: somehow or other Torrig learnt how to shape saddles; he learnt their prices; and he learnt the secret of salesmanship.

The discords ended.

And one evening, Krikor-the-Saddler invited a few of their acquaintances to his house; he offered them some rakki; he called Torrig, stood him by his side, slapped him on the face and said:

'You are a master now: I have nothing more to say!'

Torrig went almost mad with joy.

'Well, well! My Torrig has made it! If one of us lays down his head now, we have got Torrig,' said Tourvanda Korro and kissed him on the cheek which had received the slap.

Time slipped by, as it always does.

It so happened that Krikor-the-Saddler died: it was neither through a long illness nor through wearing himself out at work; but one day, he returned home from the shop and said:

'I am shivering all over, Tourvandig.'

Tourvanda Korro put him to bed, wrapped his feet up with a woollen blanket and put a hot brick in the bed; but on the following morning, Krikor-the-Saddler was no more: he had settled his accounts with the world.

'Don't cry, Auntie Tourvan; as long as I am alive, you will be a

mother to me: I'll look after you as I would a sensitive plant!'
Torrig consoled his aunt.

Tourvanda Korro embraced Torrig, crying bitterly, and she
whispered in his ear:

'Take out Krikor Agha's gold tooth, it might come in useful,
child.'

Torrig managed to keep the customers of the shop, and no
business was lost; the only difference was that before there were
two pairs of hands at work instead of one pair now.

'There were three mouths to feed before, now there are only
two,' said Tourvanda Korro.

Tourvanda Korro and Torrig would recall Krikor-the-Saddler
only when the new crops of watercress, parsley, marjoram, or
cucumber, were in season, because the old Saddler used to be fond
of them and would bring some home when they appeared in the
market.

'Krikor Agha used to eat greens like a cow,' Tourvanda Korro
would say.

'If there were cucumbers about, he would give his life for them,'
Torrig would join in.

That was how Krikor-the-Saddler's memory remained alive at
home.

While in the shop, all the customers would remember him every
time they brought their donkeys to have a new saddle made or the
old one repaired.

'They brought in five donkeys today, and all five saddles had
been made by Krikor Agha,' Torrig would inform Tourvanda
Korro.

Tourvanda Korro would have in readiness not more than two
or three tears very near to her eyes and when necessary she would
suspend them from her eyelids.

It was with piety and with deep gratitude that Torrig had paid
the priest for the grave; and he would be present personally in the
cemetery on every All Souls' Day and would have Krikor-the-
Saddler's bones blessed.

Tourvanda Korro kept her husband's clothes in the chest for a
long time, but some women acquaintances advised her that if she
gave them to Torrig to wear, he would love her even more; so
she brought them out of the chest and gave them to him. The most
valuable article out of these was the cummerbund, which Torrig
would wear with pride.

'May the good fortune of the departed soul be yours, child!' said Tourvanda Korro when Torrig turned round and round in the middle of the room to wind the cummerbund about his waist.

Time left no sharp edges of sorrow. Torrig wore out Krikor-the-Saddler's clothes, except for the precious cummerbund, while Tourvanda Korro began to think about getting Torrig married.

Every woman who undertakes to marry off a member of her family begins from the top.

Tourvanda Korro did the same.

'Torrig, my child, I will go tomorrow to ask the manufacturer's middle daughter for you,' said Tourvanda Korro.

'Hee, hee, hee...!' laughed Torrig.

Torrig was in an agitated state the whole day long, and he did not sleep a wink that night: he had once seen the manufacturer's daughter, that 'bundle of light' as he had himself called her.

Tourvanda Korro naïvely kept knocking on the big door of the manufacturer's house for a long time and waited there stubbornly.

'They don't seem to have heard me,' she thought to herself every time she knocked.

But she suddenly heard some grumbling noises.

She waited a little, the grumbling gradually seemed diabolic to her. She raised her eyes and saw a head which instantly withdrew from the window above the door, and the grumbling was resumed.

An icy perspiration enveloped Tourvanda Korro.

'Oh, my poor self...!'

If only the ground would open and swallow her up. Her feet moved; she wanted to run and get away from there as quickly as possible, but she could barely stand up.

Had Tourvanda Korro looked round, she would have seen a few heads thrust out of the window, laughing away at her.

She had hardly turned the first corner before she leant against the wall.

When Torrig heard of the incident, he said:

'My heart wasn't in it, Auntie Tourvan, but I didn't want to go against what you said.'

Tourvanda Korro was not discouraged, however: a few days later, she was again seized with the enthusiasm of finding a girl for Torrig, but this time she tried a slightly lower level.

'There's a girl who has taken my fancy, but I don't know if you
would want her or not,' said Tourvanda Korro.

'Who is it?'

'Kirakoss Effendi Yenkoyan's daughter.'

'The younger one?' asked Torrig and sensed a bird flutter inside
his heart.

'No, the elder one.'

'She's not bad either.'

The Yenkoyans received Tourvanda Korro, but this time she
did not dare mention why she had called, for their reception was
so icy and supercilious. A more difficult situation was created here
for Tourvanda Korro: what was she to say; why had she gone
to this house where she had never set foot before? All her underwear became soaked in sweat. Finally, she said:

'I have come to say that if you have any work to be done, there
is a poor woman I know with an orphan, who would be glad to
do it; and she is very clean.'

Yenkoyan Kirakoss Effendi's wife promised that if she did have
any work, she would give it to that woman.

Tourvanda Korro pulled her shawl on to her head and went
out of the house.

'Oh, what would I have done if I hadn't thought of saying
that?' she concluded on her return home.

But Torrig was unable to put himself in his aunt's place.

'If you had told them, it would have worked out,' he said.

'They all had such long faces, they would have rubbed mine in
the mud,' protested Tourvanda Korro.

Barely a week had passed when Tourvanda Korro found a new
girl. This one was neither the daughter of a manufacturer nor of a
landowner, but of a middling merchant.

'Well, Torrig, shall I go and ask them?' inquired Tourvanda
Korro.

'They wouldn't turn you down, would they?' replied Torrig
doubtfully.

'No!'

This time Tourvanda Korro dared to ask for Ignat Agha's
daughter, but returned home deeply hurt.

'They turned you down, eh?' said Torrig.

'I wish that was all they had done.'

'What did they say?' asked Torrig, interested but trembling at
the probable reply.

'What was the woman to say?'

Torrig remained silent. Inwardly, he was anxious to know what had happened but, outwardly, he assumed indifference. Tourvanda Korro continued:

' "I thought you had come to ask if you could do our laundry for us," was what she said.'

It was the first time that Torrig let out a vulgar insult directed at Ignat Agha's wife, to which Tourvanda Korro echoed:

'From me, too!'

Tourvanda Korro and Torrig went lower still down the scale, stopping at the tradespeople. Convinced that any one of them in their town would agree readily and with pleasure to give his daughter in marriage to Torrig, they sat and discussed the selection in detail and at length.

'There is Simon-the-Baker's daughter!'

'She is all right, but she is short,' objected Torrig.

'There is Ogassap-the-Builder's daughter, the little one!'

'She is all right, but I don't like her blonde hair!'

'Then there is Astour-the-Butcher's daughter!'

'She sticks out a little.'

'What about Toross-the-Shoemaker's eldest one?'

'Hee, hee, hee...!' laughed Torrig.

Tourvanda Korro pulled her shawl on to her head and went straight to Toross-the-Shoemaker's house.

The eldest daughter, Loussintak, served the coffee to Tourvanda Korro.

'Just look at my Loussintak, how she has grown...!' praised Tourvanda Korro and led up to the subject.

'Don't talk about that, Tourvanda Korro: I won't have my daughter married until she has finished her school,' replied the mother and had such a face after that, that Tourvanda Korro bade her goodbye and left.

Following Toross-the-Shoemaker, one after the other, without consulting Torrig, Tourvanda Korro called at the houses of Astour-the-Butcher, Ogassap-the-Builder, and Simon-the-Baker, and she received replies of refusal from all of them. Ogassap-the-Builder was even offensive:

'Torrig is a bit of a cow,' he said.

Apart from these tradespeople, they prepared a list of other tradespeople, and Tourvanda Korro visited all their houses, one after the other, and again received replies of refusal each time.

Torrig was extremely annoyed by these failures and he cursed each one who refused to give him his daughter.

The matter of finding a girl for Torrig became a topic of conversation for the neighbours also. Tourvanda Korro would go to them and naïvely tell them who gave her what reply, thinking that they would all side with her and curse the fortunes of each girl.

She had come to one conclusion:

'He is an orphan and has no luck,' she would say.

One of the neighbours went to Tourvanda Korro one day and said:

'I have found a girl for your Torrig, Tourvanda!'

'You don't say!'

'Her milk is pure and she is a bashful girl.'

'Tell me, who is it?'

'Ovakim's daughter.'

Tourvanda Korro's body went prickly all over: she knew whom the other had meant, but she pretended not to know.

'Which Ovakim?' she asked.

'Don't you know who Ovakim is, dear?'

'Do you mean Ghazaros-the-Poor...?'

There was silence. They used to call Ovakim 'Ghazaros-the-Poor' because of his extreme poverty; he had five daughters, all of them pretty, and he lived by a highly despicable occupation: he was a cleaner of latrines.

'I didn't expect that from you!' said finally Tourvanda Korro, without hiding her feelings: she was offended that her neighbour had proposed Ghazaros-the-Poor's daughter for Torrig.

'Tourvanda Korro,' began the neighbour, 'put aside those airs, Ghazaros-the-Poor's daughters are prettier than the manufacturer's.'

'They are angels, I suppose!'

'Don't be like that; you want a daughter-in-law and there aren't any better ones: they have turned you down everywhere!'

Tourvanda Korro did not reply and looked at her with feeble disdain.

There was silence again. Tourvanda Korro was simply waiting for her neighbour to leave, and she did.

That evening, Tourvanda Korro told Torrig about this conversation.

Torrig said:

'Is that what I am worth that I must marry Ghazaros-the-Poor's daughter?'

'You tell me...!'

But time was flying.

Torrig's dreams were troubled by a girl's white arms. Even his blanket felt the whole torment of his inflamed body. Torrig would throw the blanket away from him, he would sit up in bed and would smoke and smoke endlessly. Gradually, he persuaded himself that even one of Ghazaros-the-Poor's daughters would do; but Tourvanda Korro resisted stubbornly against it. She had announced everywhere that she would rather strangle Torrig than allow Ghazaros-the-Poor's daughter to enter her house as a daughter-in-law. Tourvanda Korro did not sense the young man's fire inside him. She had not herself experienced that fire: she was fifteen years of age when they had given her in marriage to Krikor-the-Saddler, who was then a lively young man, with a big moustache, a hoarse voice, and reddened eyes, and who had set her on fire before her own fire had started to blaze.

'Even if you hanged me, I wouldn't accept Ghazaros-the-Poor's daughter,' declared Tourvanda Korro.

Torrig was silent: it was unheard of for any man to arrange the matter of his own marriage himself even if he were in love.

But when Tourvanda Korro saw that Torrig began to break the crockery through his nervousness, that he would sometimes not come home at night, she yielded and promised to go and humble herself before Ghazaros-the-Poor.

'Tourvanda Korro,' said Ovakim-the-Latrine-cleaner's wife, 'we haven't got any girls for marriage.'

'Bah! What's this? You were going to marry off three of your five daughters long ago!'

'Three of them are already engaged,' replied Ovakim's wife proudly.

Tourvanda Korro jeered in response:

'A chicken sees millet in its dreams!'

Ovakim's wife was furious:

'There is no dreaming of millet in this; you will be seeing the trayfuls of sweet pastries turn up in a day or two!'

'What's your last word, eh?'

'My last word is: I have no daughters for your Torrig. What sort of a boy is he anyway: a saddler! Pshaw...!'

Tourvanda Korro, her eyes almost moist, left the house of Ghazaros-the-Poor. She was consumed with rage and shame. She quarrelled with two of her neighbours by the evening, uttering words they had not heard her use during the twenty years of their acquaintance.

On the very next day, Torrig stopped Ghazaros-the-Poor and said:

'I want you to come and clean out our latrine in a day or two!'

Ghazaros-the-Poor did not reply, frightened of a probable brawl that might ensue.

A few days later, somebody else also asked him to clean out their latrine; Ghazaros-the-Poor answered proudly:

'I am sorry, but you must clean out your latrine yourself; your nose won't fall off!'

The prospective client was astounded. What had happened to Ghazaros-the-Poor, had he gone mad? About ten days earlier, when Ovakim had returned home and had seen that one of his neighbours had employed a man from another quarter to clean out the latrine of their house, Ovakim had approached his colleague and had said:

'Aren't you ashamed to come and take my bread away from me?'

The secret was soon revealed.

A young man on a visit from America had become engaged to one of Ghazaros-the-Poor's daughters; he had arranged for two more of them to be married to two cousins of his in America, where he would be returning shortly, promising not only to take the remaining two sisters with him also, but the parents as well.

The young man from America had counted out two hundred dollars into Ghazaros-the-Poor's palm and had said:

'Father, from now on, you must put your feet up and rest; there is no need for you to work any more: we have a lot of money, and everything is all right!'

While Tourvanda Korro stubbornly repeated everywhere:

'They fell to my feet so many times, they begged and prayed so much that I might ask one of them for my Torrig, but I wouldn't!'

When it reached Torrig's ears that his aunt was spreading about such lies, he said:

'Auntie Tourvan, what's the good of these lies to anybody? You can see for yourself, I have no wife!'

Tourvanda Korro was unable to give a reply.

And Torrig ate his heart out particularly when the young American-Armenian had Ghazaros-the-Poor's daughters dressed up and brought them out into the street, as in America.

While Ghazaros-the-Poor went about in European clothes, with his collar and cuffs starched. And when he went past Torrig's house, Tourvanda Korro was torn with jealousy.

'Look at his moustache! He sold his daughters and look at what he has turned into!' she muttered.

'Why do you say, "sold them"?' retorted Torrig. 'The man simply had his daughters engaged. If you had been brave, you could have had one of them.'

'What are you saying, child?' said Tourvanda Korro, with fury.

'Look into my eyes, Auntie Tourvan: cut your tongue off and sit on it, we have made a mess of this business; go and find a girl if you can now!'

'I'll find one, don't you worry!' replied Tourvanda Korro, but she had a great fear in her heart that there was no more hope left. Secretly from Torrig, she had gone the day before to ask for yet another girl, and she had received a terrible reply:

'Have you come to ask the hand of a girl for a donkey? We have no daughters for donkeys!'

One morning, Torrig stood gloomily in front of his shop. He had no desire to open it; his feet were turned towards the tavern, but he thrust the key into the padlock automatically, from force of habit. He had hardly gone inside, when someone came and stood before him and said:

'Torrig...!'

'Better leave me alone; my heart is like a lump of lead!' interrupted Torrig.

But again, when from force of habit he had sat in front of a saddle and had hardly pushed the bodkin into it, one of his friends came in and exclaimed:

'Morning, Torrig!'

Torrig barely greeted back.

'Why have you got your ears hanging down like a donkey again?'

'Don't ask!'

'I'll tell you something that'll please you.'

Torrig raised his eyes.

'Have you heard?' began his friend.

'Heard what?' asked Torrig, interested, and put down the bodkin.

'There are some prostitutes visiting the town!'

'Prostitutes...?'

'Three of them!'

Torrig made some kind of a noise.

'They're so lovely; just like bundles of light!'

'Have you seen them...?'

'No, but those who have say so.'

There was complete silence.

Torrig had been unable to visualize what prostitutes were like; he had heard a great deal about them, but he had not been able to form a clear picture of them.

'Let's go tonight, eh?' said the friend.

Torrig laughed strangely, just as if a sheep had suddenly taken to laughing.

'Have you got any money?' asked the friend.

'Oh yes, plenty!' proudly replied Torrig.

'Let's go then, eh?'

Torrig did not answer and looked at his friend in a pathetic way.

'Wait under Aghanikian's Tree tonight; I'll come too, and we'll go together.'

'Where are they?'

'In the Lower Quarter.'

Torrig went to the back of the shop, behind the saddles piled up one above the other, and called his friend there. They drank a glass of rakki each.

'A-ah-h-h! It has gone right down to my toes!' said the friend.

The friend left, repeating that they would meet under Aghanikian's Tree.

Torrig sat in front of the half-finished saddle, took up the bodkin, but he was unable to proceed with his work: in the small world of his mind, extraordinary pictures were formed, each more colourful than the other, each more terrifying.

'How are you, Torrig?' asked someone.

There was no reply. Torrig had not heard anything; he was immersed in some strange imagination which was not consistent: now it would be of a happy, elevated mood, now of a spine-tingling fear, the fear of a possible prospect of its spreading in the town.

Prostitutes...! The very thought terrified him!

Torrig remembered how they had disgraced that teacher from Constantinople, Mister Bournazian, spitting into his face as they paraded him about the streets; how they had caught One-legged Artin and had forced him to run away from the town in the middle of the night; and many far worse incidents: the list was very long. But none of these dismayed Torrig.

That night, a human shadow approached Aghanikian's Tree.

'Who is it?' someone called out.

'It's me, Torrig.'

'You're late, chum!'

Torrig took hold of his friend's hand.

All was silent.

'Let's go, we're late!'

'Wait a little.'

Torrig did not feel himself on firm ground; his whole body was in flight, the fragment of some unknown song repeated in his brain.

'Let's go!'

His friend pushed Torrig forward, almost by force.

And at midnight two human shadows slid out from under Aghanikian's Tree and headed towards the Lower Quarter.

'Where to?'

'The Lower Quarter; that's where the women are.'

Torrig was seized with trembling; he stopped his friend, produced a small bottle of rakki from the folds of his sash and handed it to his friend. The latter lifted it high to his mouth and returned it to Torrig, who also took a draught from it.

'A-ah-h-h! It has gone right down to my toes!' his friend said once more.

They went forward again.

The night was immeasurably peaceful and soft. They went past thorny bushes, the honeyed fragrance from whose flowers swelled out Torrig's nostrils, and he inhaled deeply and greedily. In this serenity, only Torrig's heart was turbulent, like the roaring river which flowed below the Lower Quarter itself.

'Is it far?'

'We're nearly there.'

Torrig looked at the sky, which had grown lower: the stars were just above their heads, they were smiling.

The friend stopped in front of a small cottage; only two of its windows were dimly lit with a yellow light.

'There, that's the women's house!'

'No, really...!'

Torrig turned to stone where he stood.

'They are awake.'

'How do you know?'

'The light is still on.'

The friend went to one of the windows and gently tapped on a pane.

There was silence.

Torrig went to his friend and said:

'Let's go back!'

'Don't be an ass!'

The friend tapped on the window again.

'Oh, I hope it isn't the wrong place!'

Without taking any notice, the friend knocked once more, but a little more loudly this time.

All of a sudden, and with extreme caution, the cottage door was slowly half-opened.

Torrig's heart flew out.

The friend went to the door. They whispered something.

'Hi, Torrig, come on!'

Torrig did not know how his feet slid towards the door. They entered a dark hall and the door was shut. In the darkness someone took hold of Torrig's hand. It was not his friend, for it was a soft, small hand which had grasped his.

Suddenly the hall was partially lit when the door to the lighted room was opened.

A partly unclothed girl had opened the room-door; she had golden hair, a white skin, and was slightly built.

Inside the room there was a third girl, who was stretched out on the bed.

'How many are there?' asked this last one.

'Two,' replied the girl who had opened the front door.

'Oh well, I can go to sleep then,' she said and turned over to the wall.

Torrig was standing in the middle of the room and everything seemed to him to be veiled in a mist. His heart was quivering like a sparrow in the cage of his chest.

The girl with the golden hair approached him, held him by the arm, led him to her bed and sat him on it. His friend and the girl who had opened the front door sat on the other bed.

When Torrig sat on the girl's bed, it was as if he had flown on to the billow of a white cloud. The girl raised herself and sat on Torrig's knees.

Torrig did not know how he put his arm round this golden-haired girl's waist and squeezed it.

It was the first time that he was in such close contact with a woman; the first time that a woman's breath caressed his face; the first time that the fragrance peculiar to a woman troubled his nostrils. That fragrance was fresher than that of the yellow flowers of the thorny bushes. With his firm, coarse arms round the girl's waist, he wanted to say, 'I love you', but the words choked in his throat and, instead, he said:

'Do you like apples?'

'Yes, I do.'

'Let me go and get you some,' suggested Torrig with sincerity and warmth.

'No, no, you don't want to do that,' interrupted the girl.

'I'll go and get some!'

'You'll go and not come back any more.'

'I, not come back any more? Whatever corner of the world you go to, I will come after you,' exclaimed Torrig from his heart.

The girl believed him sincerely. There was both simplicity and depth in his words.

'Do you believe me?' asked Torrig.

'I believe you,' replied the girl and embraced him.

He kissed her.

That kiss set Torrig aflame, every particle in his body was on fire. He wanted to talk, there was a great deal in his heart which he wanted to pour out, but his tongue failed him; he looked at the girl's languid, blue eyes, her red, painted lips, her golden hair, and he embraced her with frenzy.

'Torrig, boy, what's she like, eh?' his friend suddenly asked.

'What a question!' replied Torrig and again kissed the girl.

The friend and the other girl laughed coarsely.

Torrig was annoyed.

'Why do you laugh? I wouldn't change this girl for one from heaven!'

'A girl from heaven? Huh!' exclaimed the friend, with sarcasm.

Torrig did not reply and turned to the girl. She smiled at him. There was in that smile both complaisance and irony. Others had made the same observation. But Torrig was looking at her with flaming eyes, his lips were trembling; he wanted to say something, but he could not.

After a long silence, he whispered to the girl:

'What is your name?'

'Angèle.'

'Angèle?'

'Yes.'

Torrig had never heard such a name before.

'I didn't quite get it,' he whispered.

'Angèle.'

The girl sensed his surprise. She thought that he did not believe her.

'Do you know what Angèle means?'

'Hee, hee, hee...!' laughed Torrig. 'I have never heard it before.'

'It means "angel".'

'Angel?'

'Yes.'

'It is right! You are a real angel. I believe it now!'

'I don't tell lies.'

'No, my dear, angels never tell lies.'

Angèle squeezed Torrig.

'Let me go and get you something to eat,' Torrig suggested again.

'Oh, no.'

'Yes, I will,' insisted Torrig.

'Another time.'

'Another time? What other time? I am taking you to our house.'

'Your house? Why?'

'I want to get you out of these ways. It is a shame to let you go on like this.'

At these words, Angèle's languid, blue eyes were filled with limpid tears.

'What're you making the girl cry for?' his friend reprimanded him.

'Don't stick your nose into this business!' Torrig threatened him and, turning to Angèle, he whispered, 'Don't cry, my angel; I'll take you home and look after you like a princess!'

Angèle sensed the sincerity and the delicacy of feeling in this rough, big-boned man, and she threw her arms round his neck with warmth and tenderness.

Torrig stroked her cheeks. His hands felt like a coarse brush, but her heart quivered from that caress.

'I have an aunt, who lives at my house; there is no one else,' whispered Torrig.

'What if your aunt doesn't want me there?' said the girl doubtfully.

'What's it got to do with her?' proudly replied Torrig and continued, 'It's my house! Get all your things together and let's go home.'

'Leave it until the morning.'

'No, I am going to take you back tonight; I don't want you to stay here any more.'

The girl was beset by doubts. Where would she go with this stranger? Perhaps he would take her away, maltreat her until the morning and then let her go...

'Where is your house?' asked Angèle, in order to arrest the thoughts which rushed into her brain.

'Do you know the big fountain? It's on the opposite side.'

'Let's go in the morning.'

'No, we are going now! Get up and collect your things!'

'It'll be a nuisance to your aunt if we go by night.'

'When my Aunt Tourvan sees you, she'll go mad! Come on, let's go!'

Angèle did not reply; she could not dispel the waves of doubt in her brain, although there was no fear in her heart.

'If you like, you can sleep in my aunt's bed for tonight,' suggested Torrig, 'and in the morning we can go to the priest and get married.'

Immediately, Angèle stood up, pulled out a suitcase from under the bed, put some underwear in it, and dragged on her coat and put on a hat.

'Where're you going, dearie?' asked the other girl.

Torrig answered in her place:

'To our house.'

The girl and his friend were astounded.

'What are you looking like a couple of lunatics for? She is my wife!'

When Angèle heard this daring and frank declaration, she took hold of his arm and put her head to his chest.

Torrig embraced her, lifted her up and said:

'Fly, my angel!'

Angèle went to her sleeping friend and kissed her for the last time. The girl started, thinking that a customer had arrived for her also, but when she saw Angèle with hat and coat on she was astonished.

'Where are you going?'

'To our house,' replied Torrig and picked up Angèle's suitcase.

Angèle and the other girl also kissed each other.

'Come and see us again,' said the latter.

'No, she won't come here any more, if you don't mind,' replied Torrig.

In the darkness of the street, Angèle nestled against Torrig and asked:

'Are we going straight to your house?'

'You must say "our house".'

'Our house,' repeated Angèle and put her hand on his chest.

Her heart was striving to fly out. Once more, she was beset by opposing feelings: happiness and some kind of fear which proceeded from the uncertain, the unknown situation.

'No, this rough, uncouth man would not deceive me,' she repeated mentally and walked clinging to Torrig.

'If you get tired, tell me and I will put you on my shoulder and carry you home that way.'

'No, I won't get tired,' replied Angèle.

The sky had grown lower still; the stars seemed to be pouring down into their eyes. It seemed to Torrig that the fragrance from the flowers of the thorny bushes was Angèle's own fragrance: fresh and enchanting.

Tourvanda Korro was asleep when Torrig lit the lamp and called out:

'Auntie Tourvan, get up, I have brought a wife!'

Tourvanda Korro jumped up from her bed and with sleepy eyes she saw Angèle, who was standing at the door, trembling.

'What did you say?' exclaimed Tourvanda Korro and rubbed her eyes to dispel her sleep.

'Look at my wife, look!'

Angèle, like a bird seized with fear, looked at Tourvanda Korro, with her languid, blue eyes.

'My! She looks like an angel!'

'Her name is angel also,' proudly declared Torrig.

Tourvanda Korro embraced Angèle and kissed her audibly.

'We are hungry, Auntie Tourvan, give us something to eat.'

Tourvanda Korro ran out hurriedly.

'Sit down, my angel. There, this house is yours; it's all yours, all of it!' said Torrig.

Angèle looked round at the clean, modest room and began to cry.

'Why are you crying?' asked Torrig, stroking her golden hair with his coarse hands.

'I am happy, that is why I am crying,' she replied, sobbing.

'Don't cry, my lamb, don't cry; you mustn't cry from now on. As long as I am alive, your eyes will not see any tears.'

Tourvanda Korro came in and, seeing Angèle's tears, she turned to Torrig and reprimanded him:

'Did you say something to the girl?'

'No, Auntie Tourvan, I didn't say anything; she says, "I am happy, that is why I am crying".'

Tourvanda Korro went to Angèle, took her head into her arms, pressed it to her bosom and said:

'Don't cry, my pet, don't cry. You seem to be an orphan; my Torrig was one also and I became his mother; I will be your mother, too!'

And so, after midnight, Torrig and Angèle ate bread and cheese, boiled eggs, yoghourt, greens; while Tourvanda Korro sat opposite them, her hands folded across her abdomen, looking at Angèle with wonderment and motherly tenderness.

'There isn't another like Auntie Tourvan in all the world; she is the only one,' said Torrig.

'It looks like it,' echoed Angèle, looking at Tourvanda Korro and giving her a ruby-like smile.

Then Tourvanda Korro stood up, changed Torrig's bed-clothes; took her mattress into the other room, came back, cleared the table, and said:

'Torrig, my child, your angel looks tired; go to bed.'

'Yes, my angel is tired.'

Before long, Torrig put out the lamp, and the rustling of a woman's clothing was heard, at the sound of which Torrig was barely able to hold back the bird striving to fly out of his heart.

2

In the morning, Torrig woke up early; he saw Angèle there, with her golden hair strewn over the pillow like the rays of the morning sun; he gazed at her open pink arms. She opened her eyes, which sparkled like little, cool mountain-lakes.

'It is still early, my sweet; you go on sleeping.'

Angèle turned over and closed her eyes. Walking on tiptoe, Torrig went out of the room, to let the girl sleep as much as she wanted.

Tourvanda Korro was busy in the kitchen.

'What are you doing, Auntie Tourvan?' asked Torrig.

'I am making some halva, child; I am making it for your blue-eyed wife.'

Torrig embraced his Aunt Tourvan zestfully and pressed her to his bosom.

'Did you see what a girl I found?'

'Where did you get such an angel from, child?'

Torrig need never have told Tourvanda Korro, she might never have heard anything about it, but he did not hide any of it and told her in his coarse, direct way.

'Oh, my! How I wish I had gone blind and never seen her!' exclaimed Tourvanda Korro and beat her knees.

Torrig was shaken.

'What's the matter, Auntie Tourvan?' he asked, feeling crushed.

'Oh, my child, I wish you had killed me first and then done this thing!' replied Tourvanda Korro.

Torrig could not understand her; he was completely blinded by love.

'I wouldn't exchange the manufacturer's daughter for my wife's finger-nail!'

'Don't say that, child, don't say that. How am I to look people in the face now? Oh, I will go and lie next to your Krikor Agha!'

'Auntie Tourvan, she is an orphan like myself,' whispered Torrig in a deeply moving and tremulous voice.

Angèle woke up, went out of the room and found Tourvanda Korro and Torrig sitting gloomily in the hall. She ran and embraced Torrig's head. Tourvanda looked at her with loathing, but Torrig picked the girl up, put her on his shoulder, and walked round the hall.

'She is like a bird, she is so light!'

Angèle jumped down from Torrig's shoulder, went to Tourvanda Korro, put her head upon her bosom and whispered:

'Mama Tourvan, you are Torrig's aunt, but you are my mother.'

Those words moved Tourvanda Korro; she kissed Angèle, but was unable to say anything.

A little later, when Torrig and Angèle had eaten the halva, Torrig said:

'Let's go and get married!'

Angèle followed Torrig silently.

'You need a certificate, blessed one,' said the priest.

'Oh now, priest, don't go into such details,' replied Torrig and slipped a silver mejidieh coin of twenty kouroush into his palm.

'...and let the two be one body and one soul...!' read the priest.

'One body and one soul; that's just right!' exclaimed Torrig, while Angèle silently and timorously kissed the silver cross.

When they returned home, Tourvanda Korro said to Torrig:

'It is midday, child, aren't you going to the shop?'

'I am not,' he replied and looked at Angèle with yearning.

'You mustn't stay away from your shop,' said Angèle amiably.

'What about you?'

'I will help Mama Tourvan until you come home.'

'You won't go somewhere else?' asked Torrig, with heartfelt anxiety.

Angèle understood his meaning; she went to him, kissed him, and said:

'I won't go anywhere else till I die; I am yours.'

'My angel, my lamb, my sweet...!'

Torrig ran to his shop.

When Tourvanda Korro and Angèle began doing the housework, the latter asked:

'What work does Torrig do?'

'He is a saddler,' replied Tourvanda Korro and carefully watched Angèle to see what effect this had on her.

Angèle listened indifferently.

'Are you glad?' finally asked Tourvanda Korro.

'Why not?'

Tourvanda Korro did not believe her. Angèle noticed the doubt on her face.

'Every trade is respectable, Mama Tourvan,' she said.

Torrig was unable to stay in the shop for long; he asked his neighbour to keep an eye on it and himself went home.

'Let me go and see what my angel is doing,' he thought to himself.

Angèle had taken everything out of the room and was washing the floor, her golden hair was tied up in a white cloth and her feet were bare.

'What are you doing, my angel?' asked Torrig as he went inside.

'I am washing the floor of our room,' she said and smiled.

'Bless your little feet!' said Torrig and bent down and kissed them.

She lifted him up, clung to his lips and said:

'Torrig, my soul...!'

When he went to the door to return to the shop once more, she looked at him and whispered:

'Do you mind if I change the room round a little?'

'The whole of this house is yours, you can do what you like with it; whatever you do, suits me.'

Angèle fluttered about.

In the evening, when Torrig returned home, he hardly recognized the place, in spite of the fact that not a single piece of new furniture had been added or a single object replaced: it had all been rearranged in a more practical and pleasing way.

Torrig gazed at his home with wonderment for a long time and he felt that the light which had dawned in his soul on the previous day had now broadened out even more.

'My angel,' he said with sincerity, 'you have tired yourself, you must go to bed early tonight.'

Without feigning, Angèle reassured him that she was not in the least tired and that if there were more work she could go on all night. Torrig did not believe her, because he was totally unable to imagine the consuming exhaustion and spiritual depression she had suffered when she was compelled to receive new customers every night.

The days flew past like doves for Angèle and Torrig, but hideous rumours were spread about the town.

'Have you heard, Torrig-the-Saddler has taken home a whore?'

And they would point out Torrig. Even his friend who had been responsible for his meeting Angèle had severed his relationship with Torrig.

'As soon as he saw the woman, he picked her up like a cat does a kitten in its mouth and took her home,' he told everybody.

Although Tourvanda Korro remained silent, 'sat on her tongue' as she put it, she was unable to reconcile with the terrible fact that her daughter-in-law was a prostitute! It was horrifying! For months she would not go to the bath-house, the market, or the church, and she would not visit any of her acquaintances.

'I will stay at home until God calls me to Him,' Tourvanda Korro would say.

Angèle would not go out of the house either; day and night she would occupy herself with housework, so that the defamation would not grow more intense. But Torrig did not care, he would wander about the town proudly, with his fez tilted on to his forehead.

'Whose daughter isn't immoral, tell me, eh?' he would say. 'Didn't Yenkoyan's middle daughter get herself into trouble? Didn't they do the same to Demirjoglonts's daughter? Which ones shall I name, eh? Didn't Sirma Hanoum's daughter have a brat from the servant? Didn't Chavoushian Kerop Agha's daughter-in-law go off with the coachman, eh? Which ones shall I name?'

All these were true, but none of them was defamed.

One day, Angèle cried and said:

'Torrig, my priceless one, let me go to another town so that you will be freed from these slanders.'

'What are you talking about? Are you mad? You are like a saint for me, as sacred as the Madonna!'

Angèle clung to Torrig tightly.

In a short period of time, Torrig's home was more and more transformed: curtains were hung at the windows; all the chairs and divans were covered with white sheets; the walls were white-washed; the doors and the shutters of the windows were painted; the floor of the hall was boarded; flower-pots were placed in every corner in the house and shone every morning with their many-coloured flowers; in the small, very small and neglected back-garden, flower-beds were made, which lit up with flowers. Torrig's appearance was radically changed: his moustache now neatly curved up like two commas on either side of his nose, instead of drooping over his mouth; his oriental baggy-trousers were replaced by modern, European ones; his vividly coloured waistcoat with its floral designs was replaced by a white shirt complete with collar and cuffs.

All this was brought about by Angèle, through her ingenuity and good taste.

Angèle was virtuous in the broad sense of the word: no woman on earth had been as faithful to her husband as Angèle was, that girl with the languid, blue eyes and the golden hair.

As the slander multiplied outside, so did the sense of gratitude within her deepen towards Torrig-the-Saddler, that rough and uncouth man.

'I would do anything for you, Torrig, my soul; you saved me from those ways!' Angèle would say, embracing Torrig and sprinkling her joy with a few tears, which would trickle down from her eyes.

'Don't talk about those ways any more,' Torrig would say, stroking her golden hair with his rough hands: hands which had only touched bodkins, straw, and the backs of donkeys.

Torrig used to bring a present for Angèle every day, be it something very small. Even if he brought home some fruit, which he had also been in the habit of doing before he was married, he would put it in front of her and say:

'I have brought it for you, eat it, my lamb.'

Torrig was not adept with words. His adjectives did not go beyond the use of 'angel' and 'lamb', but Angèle felt that in those ordinary words there was an unbounded warmth and tenderness.

In the course of time, the slanderous mouths grew tired. The transformation of Torrig and his home, Angèle's enviable virtuousness, her good taste, her talents, converted people's minds.

'Have you seen how the prostitute has come to be a saint?' they would say.

A bride's mother-in-law would shout at her and say:

'You are not even as good as Tourvanda's daughter-in-law; her one finger is worth the whole of you!'

And in the course of time, a deep remorse was born within Tourvanda Korro towards this innocent, faithful and obedient girl, endowed with a thousand and one talents; and this remorse developed into an infinite maternal love.

One day, Angèle was washing Torrig's socks, when Tourvanda Korro came in, went to her, held her by her soapy hands, drew her to herself, put the girl's arms round her waist, herself embraced her and began to cry. Angèle realized why she was crying and felt that those tears were cooling her soul.

'My daughter-in-law, my sweet daughter-in-law, there is not one like you in the whole world: forgive me, my pet!' sobbed Tourvanda Korro.

Angèle did not reply, but she embraced her more firmly and mingled her own tears with hers.

Upon hearing this, Torrig went mad with delight.

'I have only a wife and an aunt in this world; the rest of the people are...'

Torrig jumped about and swore through joy, now embracing his wife, now his aunt.

The following morning, Tourvanda Korro said to him:

'Torrig, my pet, I am going to take my little daughter-in-law to the baths.'

Torrig was so happy that he could not speak; he looked at his aunt lengthily and with tenderness, he put out his hand towards her and said:

'Bathe her in the private room.'

When Angèle undressed herself in the baths, her body seemed to give out light: it was so pure and white.

Everyone looked at her with admiration, for beauty has no enemy. A woman even whispered in the ear of another:

'What does it matter if a woman is immoral as long as she is beautiful? We call ourselves women! Pshaw!'

Tourvanda Korro herself loosened Angèle's golden hair, which spread on to her marble shoulders, as if the sun had embraced her. When Tourvanda Korro saw that everyone was looking at her daughter-in-law, she stealthily pinched her in the soft regions. Angèle could not understand why she had done this. When they went into the private bathing-room, she asked:

'Why did you pinch me, Mama Tourvan?'

'So that no evil eye might touch you, my pet,' she replied.

Angèle smiled at her naïvety.

When they had left home, Torrig had gone straight to the market square; there he had approached the driver of a carriage whom he knew, and had asked:

'Do you know my Auntie Tourvan?'

'Who doesn't?'

'Take your carriage to Hadji Doursoun's bath-house and wait at the entrance until my Auntie Tourvan and my wife come out. Let them step into your carriage, and take them home. Hurry now! I'll pay you well for it!'

The driver had shaken the reins and the horses had flown away.

Those who came out of the bath-house saw Tourvanda Korro and Angèle sit in the carriage. An evil-minded woman, whose two daughters were still left unmarried at home, muttered some insulting words. And behind her black veil her face turned yellow with jealousy.

In the carriage, Tourvanda Korro, her head held high, wanted everyone to see her.

At home, for the first time in his life, Torrig had prepared the tea; he had brought a roast chicken and greens from the market, and a new dress for Angèle.

When Tourvanda Korro and Angèle alighted from the carriage and went inside the small house, in front of the door of which a carriage had stopped for the first time, Torrig came out, paid the driver, sent him away, and proudly looked up and down the street.

When he went inside the house, he saw Angèle with her hair still wet, her face slightly flushed from the hot water, like a pale carnation; he embraced her, lifted her on to his shoulder, and walked about in the house, through the profound happiness in his soul.

Tourvanda Korro, her hands clasped across her abdomen, watched with admiration and uncommon joy, and said:

'How I wish your Krikor Agha were alive to see this!'

'Ah yes, and my mother also!' whispered Torrig.

Tourvanda Korro suddenly began to sob, remembering her poor, unfortunate sister, on whose grave thrived daisies with their yellow buttons.

The days flew past.

Life flowed on for Torrig and Angèle like a happy stream.

The manufacturer's daughter, whose hand in marriage Tourvanda Korro had sought and had been hurt, became consumptive through her husband's drunkenness and lechery, and died.

When her coffin went past in the street, Torrig asked:

'Who has died?'

'It's that one!' replied Tourvanda Korro.

'Poor thing!' whispered Torrig and sadly withdrew from the window.

'If they had given her to you, she would now...'

'No,' Torrig cut in, 'it was a good thing they didn't.'

Every morning, before going to the shop, Torrig would instruct Tourvanda Korro:

'Don't let my lamb lift heavy things, will you, Auntie Tourvan!'

'No, my dear, I won't!'

And towards the middle of July, Angèle sat out in the back-garden, which was the size of two or three bed-sheets, opposite the pale-blue flowers which she had grown, sewing little chemises for her infant, who already wriggled beneath her heart and often struck powerful blows against its mother's abdomen, at which the mother would smile with her languid, blue eyes. Life for Angèle was the fragrance of those pale-blue flowers and the radiance of those pale-blue flowers.

A Provincial Tragedy

ON LEAVING HOME one morning, Khambourents Hadji Agha, instead of walking past Mehmet Pasha Gardens, past the Small Fountain, along the wall of the Old Church, towards the Great Square and from there to his shop, barely fifty paces beyond—a route he had unswervingly pursued for thirty-five years—after going past Mehmet Pasha Gardens, he turned into Boshayents Street, then, walking along the front of the Arsenal, he came to the Great Square and from there went to his shop.

It so happened that, while he was passing through Boshayents Street, Hadji Agha straightened up his back, raised his head, glanced at one of the windows and went on his way, with his head bent down, until he came to his shop.

When he opened the door of the shop and went inside, suddenly he, too, reflected upon the strangeness of what he had done and was puzzled why he had gone through Boshayents Street, instead of keeping to his usual route. Failing to think of an explanation, he chuckled to himself, stroked his greying moustache, and began to open the shutters of the shop.

Not having been to Boshayents Street for the previous thirty-five years, Hadji Agha was completely unaware of what changes had taken place there: who had gone away and who had moved in.

While Hadji Agha was busy serving his customers as usual, an incident was germinating in Boshayents Street: when he had straightened up his back in that street, raised his head and glanced at one of the windows, from another window immediately opposite, a woman had seen him and, stepping back, she had exclaimed in amazement:

'Oh, my! What was that about? God Almighty!'

Those inside the room, upon hearing her, had immediately and spontaneously crossed themselves and asked with even greater astonishment:

'What's happened, Elmass Hatoun?'

Paying no attention to the questions put to her, Elmass Hatoun had continued:

'O Lord! O gentle Mother of God, do not remember our sins!'

Then, spreading out her arms, she had stood in the middle of the room and muttered two verses from the hymn 'Lord have mercy upon us!'

'What has happened, Elmass Hatoun?' had asked her husband's sister-in-law.

'Send the children out and I'll tell you,' had declared Elmass Hatoun and continued mysteriously: 'Christ, O Lord, do not remember our sins!'

They had sent the children out of the room at once and the four sisters-in-law, the eldest one being Elmass Hatoun, had sat down on the rug in the corner.

Elmass Hatoun began:

'Khambourents Hadji Agha was going through our street...'

'No, really?' exclaimed the other sister-in-law, leaning close to Elmass Hatoun.

And the latter continued:

'He was standing there, staring at Aghkadents's wife!'

'No...!' exclaimed the others in unison.

'And Aghkadents's wife,' continued Elmass Hatoun, 'the stuck-up wench, knew it all right: she was behind the window.'

'No...! May God forgive her...!'

'If a man like Hadji Agha has got out of the straight path,' continued Elmass Hatoun, 'may the good Lord help him! Cross yourselves...!'

When the young goldsmith Dikran lived in another quarter of the town, they used to call him 'Dikran-the-Goldsmith'; but when he married and, with the money he had saved up, he bought a house in Boshayents Street, which was considered to be a better quarter, the inhabitants of that street would not forgive him for this climb and they began to call him 'Aghkadents'—which means 'The Poor-Ones'—as a title of contempt.

Dikran had married a poor but attractive girl. Her name was Piloun, and they would all say:

'She is just like her name, radiant, and looks like the sun!'— *Piloun* being the Armenian for 'radiant'.

Piloun's parents had died within seven days of each other; their creditors had taken away everything and sold it in settlement of her father's debts, leaving the house empty and Piloun absolutely destitute. It was at that time, barely forty days after her parents' death, that Dikran-the-Goldsmith, without resorting to a customary mediator, had approached Piloun and proposed marriage to her. The impoverished girl, filled with despair and dismay, had taken the goldsmith's hand and had gone with him without hesitation. It was two months after their marriage that Dikran had bought the house in Boshayents Street and nearly a year since he had been living there with Piloun, peacefully and happily.

On the morning when Khambourents Hadji Agha had passed through Boshayents Street and, stopping in front of Dikran's house, he had glanced at the window, Piloun had not been at home. She had gone out half an hour earlier, together with Dikran, to visit his aunt's house, where they had been invited to lunch. Dikran's aunt had told him to keep his shop shut until midday and to go to her house with Piloun in the morning. And that was what they had done.

So that, when Khambourents Hadji Agha had stopped in Boshayents Street and had glanced at one of Dikran-the-Goldsmith's windows, there had been no one at home; but it had seemed to Elmass Hatoun that 'there was a shadow behind the window' and that this must have been the young wife's shadow.

Elmass Hatoun and the two sisters-in-law immediately younger than herself, leaving the cleaning of the house and the cooking to the youngest sister-in-law, slipped their veils on to their heads and went out of the house, each in a different direction.

Elmass Hatoun, fifty steps beyond—in the very same Boshayents Street—entered a house and began:

'Oh my, Loussintak Hatoun, have you heard what's happened?'

Loussintak Hatoun, fired by her thirst for gossip, immediately abandoned her work and, infuriated by the children, exclaimed:

'Pah! Do you think my brats will let me put a foot outside the front-door and hear anything? Tell me, what's happened?'

'Khambourents Hadji Agha passed through our street...!'

'No...!' exclaimed Loussintak Hatoun, astonished.

Elmass Hatoun hastened to add:

'He had his eyes fixed on...Aghkadents's wife!'

'Piloun?'

'The stuck-up wench! She was behind the window!'

'It's less than a year since they got married and she's already got her eye somewhere else, eh?' echoed Loussintak Hatoun.

'Yes, and what about Hadji Agha? Isn't he ashamed of his white hair?' continued Elmass Hatoun.

'Oh my, my, my! How times have changed!' said Loussintak

Hatoun and stood there aghast, folding her hands across her abdomen.

Elmass Hatoun did not stay any longer: she went out, walked on and, taking the first turning, she entered another house.

'Have you heard, Tereza Hatoun?'

'No...?'

'Oh my, have you been sleeping inside a camel's ear or what?'

'Tell me now, quick, Elmass Hatoun, or I'll explode!'

'Khambourents Hadji Agha...!'

'Oh, what days these are!' exclaimed Tereza Hatoun.

Elmass Hatoun continued with her wanderings. While Tereza Hatoun, left alone, once more exclaimed:

'Oh, the wives of today! Ay-ay-ay...!'

Elmass Hatoun entered a third, a fourth and yet a tenth door, conveyed the terrible news and returned home barely in time for lunch, completely exhausted.

The other sisters-in-law had, in their turn, gone in and out of various houses. Those who had received the news, also in their turn entered other doors.

'My dear, haven't you heard how in Boshayents Street...?'

'When?'

'This morning...!'

Each listener had repeated the incident to another with a slightly different content, so that in the evening when the women told their husbands about the unusual event which had occurred in Boshayents Street, it had assumed the following form: Khambourents Hadji Agha had been seen to come out of young Dikran-the-Goldsmith's house and the young wife had also been seen to shut the door quietly behind the visitor.

The following morning, a peaceful and sunny morning in May, when Tangakin Hatoun, her large sieve heaped with roses from the garden, entered the forecourt of the house, she heard the terrible news. Her legs gave way under her: she threw away the sieve, from which the roses spilt on to the flagstones, and she was barely able to stretch out her hand to the top of a stake in the fence and save herself from collapsing to the ground.

Tangakin Hatoun was the sister of Hadji Agha's wife, Memik Hatoun.

'Where did you hear it?' asked Tangakin Hatoun, crouching.

'The whole town is talking about it, dear!'

It was nearly half an hour before Tangakin Hatoun regained her composure: whereupon, she put her shawl over her head and ran to her sister's home.

As soon as she went in, she exclaimed:

'Oh my, oh my, sister! I have heard such a terrible thing that my ear is all burnt up!'

Memik Hatoun was alarmed:

'You don't say, Tangouk!'

'Oh, Memik dear, oh! It would have been better if you hadn't come into this world!'

It did not even enter Memik Hatoun's head that what her sister had heard could possibly have any connection with her own marriage of many years' standing: she had had a daughter, whom she had married off, and she even had a grandchild.

'Quick, tell me what it is, I am feeling faint!' pleaded Memik Hatoun, shaking in all her body.

Tangakin Hatoun did not know how to begin, and she circled round the room, rubbing her hands together.

'The whole town has been set on fire with it, sister!'

'Tell me then, dear!'

'I never expected such a thing from my brother-in-law, God bless my soul!'

Memik Hatoun lost her patience.

'Hurry up and tell me, or I'll bawl my head off!'

Tangakin Hatoun told her about the incident.

'Woe me...!' screamed Memik Hatoun and slumped across the divan.

Tangakin Hatoun embraced her and made her sit up.

'You were right, sister, I wish I hadn't come into this world! I wish I had broken my leg and had not gone to church and got married! Oh, what has happened to me, what has happened to me...!'

The two sisters embraced each other and cried for a long time, mingling their tears together.

Tangakin Hatoun's story was quite different by this time. To begin with, not only had this not been the first time that Hadji Agha had passed through Boshayents Street, but there had been many such occasions; then, when he had come out of Dikran-the-Goldsmith's house, it seems that Piloun had had her arms round Hadji Agha's neck; thirdly, when the children in the street had seen him in that attitude they had shouted, 'Shame on you!', and they had disgraced him all the way to the shop.

In accordance with his custom of many years, Hadji Agha would shut his shop every evening and, after turning the key in the padlock for the last time, he would cross himself; then, in accordance with his custom of many years, he would cough and clear his throat, he would adjust the angle of his fez and would walk away. He would hang his head down as he went, his mind preoccupied with one of the unsuccessful deals of that day.

He would return home by the same route: from the shop to the Great Square, from there along the wall of the Old Church, past the Small Fountain, past Mehmet Pasha Gardens, to his house. There, in front of the house, in accordance with his custom of many years, he would stop a while, would roll a cigarette, light it and take a puff at it; he would look up the street, then down it, he would accept people's greetings and return them, and, in accordance with his custom of many years, he would knock on the door three times. His wife would at once know from the number and the loudness of the knocks that it was Hadji Agha; she would run and open the door, smile and gently whisper:

'Ah, Hadji Agha?'

And he would say:

'Memik?'

He would take off his galoshes—he used to wear galoshes both in the winter and in the summer. Then he would go upstairs to his room, where he would sit cross-legged and wait for his wife, in accordance with the custom of many years, to bring him a small tray with fifty grammes of rakki on it and a small plateful of pickles. It would take him more than an hour to drink the fifty grammes of rakki, which he would sip gradually, savouring every drop. Then Memik Hatoun would bring up the supper and they would eat together. Hadji Agha would invariably tell her some anecdote from the business activities of that day, an anecdote which would differ barely by a hair's breadth from that of the previous day, but his wife would listen as if it were a completely new one.

All this was performed with unshakeable monotony and unerring regularity, for thirty-five years, and had a single point been changed, it would have been tantamount to people suddenly finding one morning that the stonework, the windows, and the doors of a house had been rearranged in a totally different order.

On the evening of the day after Hadji Agha had gone through
Boshayents Street, when he had closed the shutters of the shop,
he went out, pushed the door to and hung up the padlock, he
seemed to sense a strangeness in the air; a few of the people who
went by gave him a curious, an altogether unusual look. Nevertheless, Hadji Agha thrust his key into the padlock, turned it and
upon pulling it out and crossing himself, in accordance with his
custom of many years, he adjusted his fez and, hanging his head
down, he walked away. As he crossed the Great Square, he raised
his head once and glanced around: it became obvious to him now
that people were looking at him with some strange interest.

'I wonder if anything has happened at home,' he thought to
himself and hurried his steps.

By hurrying his steps he had upset the regularity of years and
those who saw it made a mental note. As he went along the church
wall, Hadji Agha raised his head once more and glanced around:
this time he sensed that even the women hurrying to church were
looking at him in an unusual way from behind their veils.

'I wonder...!' muttered Hadji Agha and hurried his steps even
more.

He met many strange looks until he reached home. A passer-by
even said something which sounded like a remark directed at him
obliquely. Although he did not quite catch the words, he felt
that they bore a tone of reproach aimed at him.

At long last he reached the front door of his house. He did not,
in accordance with his custom of many years, stop there and roll a
cigarette, but he knocked on the door straightaway. In accordance
with his custom of many years, he should have knocked three
times, but he did so more than three times, an act which he performed unknowingly, as a result of his nervous state.

When there were more than three knocks on the door, Memik
Hatoun did not pay any attention, because she did not think it
could be Hadji Agha: she would open it a little later; but outside,
Hadji Agha was astounded and even frightened.

'What has happened that they won't even open the door?' he
whispered to himself and, both through impatience and unusual
concern, he knocked again.

'Who can that be?' exclaimed Memik Hatoun annoyed and
slowly went to open the door.

When she saw Hadji Agha there, she cried out with astonishment:
'Ah! Hadji Agha, it's you...?'

He was likewise astonished and hurriedly, as if someone had pushed him from behind, he stumbled inside.

'Memik...?'

This was not Hadji Agha's voice: it had lost its natural tone, it was trembling.

Memik Hatoun also became tongue-tied; she was unable to reply immediately and barely managed to rest her back against the wall, where she turned to stone with stupefied eyes.

Husband and wife looked at each other, as if they were trying to recognize one another.

'Go upstairs, go on!' Memik Hatoun suddenly whispered.

With shaking but hasty steps Hadji Agha went upstairs, thinking that he would see there whatever it was that had happened: but there was nothing in the room, it was the same as on other days and everything was in its usual place.

He rested a little and sitting on the divan in the corner, covered with oriental rugs, he waited, in accordance with his custom of many years, for his wife to bring up the tray with fifty grammes of rakki and a plateful of pickles on it.

He waited quite a while: but she did not come.

'There's something going on!' said Hadji Agha to himself and, going to the door, he called down:

'Memik...!'

Memik appeared on the stairs, tray in hand.

In accordance with the custom of many years, Memik Hatoun should have sat next to Hadji Agha and listened to an anecdote from the day's business. She did sit down, but Hadji Agha did not, contrary to his custom of many years, tell one. Suddenly there was a nervous knocking on the front door.

Memik Hatoun immediately jumped up and went down to open the door. She heard Hadji Agha say to himself:

'I wonder...!'

She opened the door and was barely able to embrace her daughter, who threw herself upon her mother's bosom crying and exclaimed:

'Oh, mother, I wish I had never heard it!'

It was obvious that the daughter had also heard the simmering gossip against her father and she had run to her mother.

Mother and daughter, in each other's arms, shed tears.

Hadji Agha heard the sound of crying and waited; but when he saw that the lamenting would not cease, he too went below.

Mother and daughter were astounded to see him, for he had heard crying many times before, but he had never moved from his place.

'Memik, Mayranoush, what is all this about?' he asked in a muffled voice.

Mother and daughter remained silent and dried their tears.

Hadji Agha roared with rage:

'Well...?'

Mayranoush expected her mother to explode and spill all her venom on to her father's head, but Memik Hatoun thought it prudent to say nothing for the present and she invented a lie there and then:

'Our son-in-law has bawled at Mayranoush.'

'All right!' muttered Hadji Agha.

Mother and daughter interpreted this remark to mean that he knew it was a lie.

Hadji Agha continued:

'He's a man, he can bawl and he can be loving, you needn't turn it into a big affair; and don't you egg your daughter on either!'

'Hadji Agha!' exclaimed Memik Hatoun reproachfully.

Hadji Agha, who had started climbing up the stairs, turned round and curtly uttered:

'He's a man!'

Mother and daughter remained silent, because the poor son-in-law was not guilty and it was a good thing that Hadji Agha felt as he did, otherwise he might turn on him and disgrace him.

Hadji Agha went upstairs, filled himself a glass of rakki, drank it and muttered:

'If he has bawled, he has bawled! And he'll do it again...!'

He sat down.

Memik Hatoun brought up the meal in due course, but she did not eat anything herself. Hadji Agha ascribed this to her being upset by the son-in-law's behaviour, but he did not say anything about it, he merely asked:

'Has Mayranoush gone?'

'She has.'

A few times, Memik Hatoun wanted to broach the subject and reveal everything, but she did not dare.

Suddenly, from below the window, a street urchin called out in a shrill voice:

'Piloun...!'

Memik Hatoun realized what this meant and she turned pale.

The street urchin again called out and in an even shriller voice: 'Piloun, girl...!'

Memik Hatoun could not stand it when she heard the cry for the second time.

'Oh, I wish I didn't have ears to hear with!' she exclaimed and slumped across the rug.

Hadji Agha could not understand any of this, he had not even heard clearly what the urchin had called out. He lifted up his wife, made her drink some water and said:

'What is all this, have you all gone mad?'

Memik Hatoun kept quiet and dried her tears; then she had enough strength to stand up, to clear away the supper things, and lay out the mattresses for the night. Hadji Agha was in the habit of going to bed very early. He prayed briefly on one knee, went to bed and fell asleep. Whereas Memik Hatoun prayed for a long time; then she went to bed, but did not sleep: she sat up in bed to see if Hadji Agha would say anything in his sleep; one word would have been enough for her to have reached a definite conclusion.

Hadji Agha slept right through the night without uttering a word and almost without moving, and in the morning he got up, in accordance with his custom of many years, at the right time, but before going to the shop, contrary to his custom of many years, he drank two glasses of rakki. Memik Hatoun recalled that, ever since they had been married, this had occurred only once before, about ten years earlier, and that had been due to a very good reason: Hadji Agha had received the news that his only sister, who lived in America, had died.

'Why did he drink again today?' Memik Hatoun asked herself, and in response she visualized before her eyes Dikran-the-Goldsmith's young wife, Piloun.

'The stuck-up wench!' she said mentally and, filled with evil, she pulled her shawl over her head and, going out through the garden gate, she walked down the street.

She wanted to ascertain secretly through which street Hadji Agha would go to the shop that day.

In accordance with his custom of many years, Hadji Agha walked past Mehmet Pasha Gardens, past the Small Fountain, along the wall of the Old Church, towards the Great Square and thence to his shop.

But Hadji Agha's going to the shop that day differed in one respect from his custom of many years: he looked around, watching those who passed him, because, as on the previous day, he caught their strange looks, so strange that he even wanted to stop one of them and ask him the reason, but he restrained himself with supreme effort.

He opened his shop and began to examine the materials, folded them up, smoothed them down, put them in their place and waited for customers to arrive. Contrary to his custom of many years, he did not derive any pleasure from busying himself with the materials. A peasant customer came in and Hadji Agha occupied himself with him eagerly: he opened out more materials than usual and let him make his choice, while he himself looked outwards. He witnessed a most unusual sight: there were a few people standing a little distance away from the shop and one of them was pointing him out with his finger to the others. The peasant customer became lost to Hadji Agha's eyes, the whole shop turned misty, but shaking himself he restored the clarity of his vision and once more occupied himself with the customer.

'It's good stuff, there is no question about it,' he said mechanically.

He did not hear the peasant's reply, because just at that moment one of the townsfolk, whom Hadji Agha knew well and with whom he did business, came and stood in front of the shop and said with sarcasm and reproach:

'Well done, Hadji Agha, well done!'

Hadji Agha wanted to call the man inside and ask him what he meant, but being slow in taking decisions the man had gone away by the time he had made up his mind.

Now Hadji Agha was curt to the peasant, who could not understand why his obliging manner of a minute earlier had suddenly changed.

'Buy what you want and go; don't be a headache!' sourly said Hadji Agha, for whom no customer had ever been too much trouble.

'There's plenty of this stuff in other shops,' said the peasant.

'Well then, if there is, go and get it from somewhere else!' bluntly retorted Hadji Agha and began to put away the materials.

The customer departed.

As Hadji Agha folded away each length of material, he kept looking outwards. Although there was no one watching him, he began to imagine that every passer-by glanced inside as he went past. He was putting the last piece of material in its place, when Markar Agha entered. Hadji Agha became extremely worried: why should Markar Agha have come to his shop at that hour of the day? For he, too, was another one of those people who would keep to his own routine of years; and Markar Agha had never before set foot in Hadji Agha's shop at that hour.

As soon as Markar Agha entered, he said:

'Let's see now, how is my Hadji Agha today?'

Hadji Agha did not reply; his tongue had instantly dried up, because he thought that Markar Agha's arrival was another of the links in the recent strange happenings.

'I said, how is my Hadji Agha today?' repeated Markar Agha.

It seemed to Hadji Agha that the other was making fun of him, and he retorted:

'For the love of God, Markar Agha, it's enough! This is no time for jokes!'

Markar Agha was astonished: he had not heard anything and was surprised that Hadji Agha was not only not pleased about his inquiring after his well-being, but also at his having called on him.

'What's the matter, are you drunk?' asked Markar Agha, half-sarcastically this time, and added, 'Don't take any notice, enjoy yourself; let them say what they like!'

'Shall I tell you something, Markar Agha?' asked Hadji Agha.

'You can tell me as many things as you like!'

'No, there is only one thing I want to know.'

'What is it?'

'What are you holding back from me?'

'Nothing, my dear friend!'

'I know you are hiding something!'

Markar Agha swore that he was not keeping anything back from him.

'Are you quite sure?'

'My dear Hadji Agha, of course I am sure!'

Markar Agha noticed that Hadji Agha was looking outwards with astonishment. He, too, looked that way: there were a few people, with their fezes tilted forward at an insolent angle and their eyes screwed up, staring at Hadji Agha. After gazing at him for quite a while, they left, whispering something to one another and chuckling away.

'Markar Agha,' uttered Hadji Agha in a trembling voice, 'what is all this?'

'What is what, Hadji Agha?'

'They all look at me.'

'What does it matter, let them look!'

'Let them look...!' drawled Hadji Agha.

'Yes, let them!'

'Markar Agha,' exclaimed Hadji Agha, irritated, 'are you a child, or an ass?'

'I am neither a child nor an ass, you idiot!' retorted Markar Agha, hurt.

There followed a silence; then Hadji Agha instantly sobered down and, realizing that he had made an unnecessary remark, he said:

'I am sorry, it was a slip of the tongue.'

'I came here to ask how you were keeping and that was what I got in return, and now you ask me to forgive you!' replied Markar Agha and left the shop without a word more.

Hadji Agha came to the conclusion that he had behaved rudely towards Markar Agha, but in the end he persuaded himself that the other had been keeping something back from him. Making a great effort, he began to occupy himself with the materials in the shop, in order to refrain from looking out into the street. He rearranged the materials which he had already put away, but he was unable to overcome his ardent inner desire and he looked outwards once more. There were a few people standing outside, gazing at him in a strange way. He realized that he would not be able to escape from these stares and a thought took shape in his mind: to shut up the shop and go home.

This time he made his decision surprisingly quickly, shut the shop rapidly, and walked away with head bent down.

Somebody at his side made a remark, which Hadji Agha did not hear:

'He's going to visit the young wife!'

And the man followed him.

Hadji Agha had crossed the Great Square and was walking along the Old Church wall, when he suddenly heard:

'Piloun, girl...!'

Again he paid no attention to these calls, as he had not done previously when they had come from below the window at his home.

'Piloun, girl...!'

It was a shrill voice and laden with mockery; it belonged to the

same street urchin: he had black eyes and cropped hair, bristly
like a brush.

Hadji Agha continued to walk.

This time the urchin stood in Hadji Agha's way, thrust two
fingers in his own mouth and emitted a piercing whistle and
called out:

'Piloun, girl...!'

With astonishing speed, like a flash of lightning that lashes
across the entire sky in an instant, Hadji Agha's thoughts were
linked up with that call from which his wife had almost fainted.

'So that "Piloun, girl!" has something to do with me,' he
thought to himself, but, unable to make any sense of it, he was
plunged into tormenting thoughts.

When the urchin called out yet once more and ran away, there
was no longer any doubt left in Hadji Agha's mind.

When his wife opened the door and saw her husband there, she
exclaimed:

'Oh, it's you, Hadji Agha?'

He swept past her and went inside.

'Are you ill?' asked his wife.

'No!'

'Why did you come home then, dear?'

'Something's happened to me, wife; the whole town is swim-
ming round my head!'

'That's what happens when a man goes and does what he hasn't
done for forty years!'

'What is that?' asked Hadji Agha anxiously.

Memik Hatoun remained silent.

Hadji Agha turned round, looked piercingly into his wife's
eyes and asked:

'Tell me what it is that you are hiding from me!'

Memik Hatoun was about to tell everything, but she heard a
call from the street and was completely transformed.

Someone had shouted:

'Piloun is waiting for you!'

'It's that name Piloun again,' thought Hadji Agha, whereas
Memik Hatoun would have sprawled on to the ground had her
husband not caught her.

Hadji Agha was unable to come to any conclusion, because he
had not known anyone, anywhere, by the name of Piloun during
the whole of his life.

'Tell me what is going on, Memik!' said Hadji Agha in a pathetic voice.

Memik Hatoun was unable to speak, her tears were choking her.

Silent and with head bowed, Hadji Agha went upstairs, gulped down two glasses of rakki and began marching about the room. He could not make any guesses; he brought to mind a thousand and one things, weighed them up, turned them inside out, but there was not a glimmer of light. After wandering about and pondering for a long time, he went below. His wife was in the kitchen. He went inside, stood before her and blurted out:

'Tell me, Memik, is it me that's gone off my head, or is it you people?'

'It's you!'

Hadji Agha turned to stone. He was not expecting such a reply. Suddenly, he shouted:

'Tell me what all this is about, will you!'

Memik Hatoun remained silent.

Hadji Agha became furious, approached his wife, seized her by the shoulders and shouted threateningly:

'Speak! Speak! Speak...!'

Memik Hatoun told him all that she had heard.

'Do you believe these things, Memik?' asked Hadji Agha, who had turned as white as a sheet.

'They had seen it all with their own eyes.'

'I am asking you if you believe it!'

Memik Hatoun thought to herself:

'Could all these things possibly have been wrong?'

Hadji Agha's eyes were awaiting a reply.

Memik Hatoun repeated:

'They had seen it all with their own eyes.'

Hadji Agha left the kitchen without another word and went to the upstairs room. Memik Hatoun took him his meal at the right time. Hadji Agha was sitting on the divan in the corner thumbing his rosary. Outwardly, he was very calm. Memik Hatoun put the meal before him and went below. Hadji Agha did not even look at it, so that when Memik Hatoun came up to collect the dishes, she saw that it had not been touched.

The whispers spreading about the town reached Dikran-the-Goldsmith's ear also.

At first he hesitated, he did not know himself where and how he came to hear about it and who it was that had first told him; but gradually it became clear to him that Khambourents Hadji Agha had gone to his house, had embraced his wife, and they had behaved so daringly and shamelessly that people outside had heard what they had said. While his wife had seen Hadji Agha off with her arms round his neck and had kissed him at the front door. And many people had seen all this with their own eyes.

Like Hadji Agha, Dikran-the-Goldsmith himself became the target of strange looks. Those looks would not let him do his work: he spoilt a few rings; the crucible of molten gold fell from his hand and completely spilt in the ashes. He had become the only cuckold in the town.

Whipped by these strange looks, Dikran would fly up, remove his leather apron, shut his workshop and go home. Piloun would meet him with warm affection, she would embrace and fondle him. Not doubting in the least his wife's sincerity and virtue, he would return to his workshop, settle down and work ardently; but the eyes that looked through the shop-window would not leave him in peace.

In order to be able to confirm his wife's intrigue, he would go home suddenly to catch Hadji Agha there. He pretended a few times that he would be going to some village or other and suddenly returned, but he failed to witness anything. He kept watch on Khambourents Hadji Agha, who would no longer go out of his house and whose shop remained shut. At first, Dikran was able to reason sanely: what motive could his young wife have to love Hadji Agha? What could she be after: he, Dikran, was young and she was not short of anything? Could Hadji Agha possibly possess any advantage over him, even to the slightest degree, for his wife not only to deceive him but to go to the extent of embracing Hadji Agha at the front door as she saw him off?

This was how Dikran-the-Goldsmith thought and argued to himself in the early days; but his consciousness gradually darkened, he began to visualize scenes of debauchery: Hadji Agha and his wife together in his own bed, or on the divan in the corner; perhaps, even in the kitchen...!

One day Dikran made a silver bracelet and sent it home as a present to his wife.

'Don't tell her I sent you, just say that it is a present from somebody,' he ordered the boy with whom he sent the bracelet.

Dikran had thought of this move, to see if Piloun would herself disclose whether she had received a present or not when he returned home that evening.

As soon as he had set foot in the house at the end of the day, Piloun went to meet him and with childlike delight she showed him her wrist. Dikran saw the bracelet and asked mysteriously:

'Did your aunt give it to you?'

'No!'

'Who did, then?'

'Wasn't it you who sent it to me?'

'No!'

'Oh...?' exclaimed Piloun. 'And I said to myself, it's from my Dikran!'

'Who brought it?'

'A boy.'

'What did he say?'

'He said it was a present.'

'Didn't you ask him who it was from?'

'No!'

'Why not?'

'Well! Why should I have asked? I knew it was you who had sent it!'

'Let's go inside and I'll have a look at it there!' said Dikran-the-Goldsmith, and together they went into the room.

There he took the bracelet off his wife's wrist, examined it closely and said:

'Piloun dear, this is my work!'

'I know, I recognized your handiwork.'

'Yes, but it wasn't me who sent it to you!'

'Who did you make it for? Try and remember!' asked Piloun.

The goldsmith looked straight into his wife's eyes and said:

'I made it for Khambourents Hadji Agha.'

'Khambourents Hadji Agha?'

'Yes!'

Piloun laughed loudly and innocently.

'What are you laughing at?' asked Dikran angrily.

'Why shouldn't I laugh, dear...? Khambourents Hadji Agha...?' drawled Piloun and again laughed loudly and asked: 'When did you make it?'

'Two days ago.'

'I can't make it out at all!' said Piloun with astonishment and went out.

Dikran thought to himself: 'I have made myself look a fool.' When he heard his wife singing and humming away, he grew furious; he went outside and said to her bluntly:

'Send the bracelet back, Piloun!'

'To whom?'

'To Hadji Agha!'

'Don't talk like an idiot!'

'You are the idiot!'

Piloun remained silent. It was the first time that there had been any cross words between them.

'Send it back now!'

'Perhaps it wasn't him who sent it to me.'

'Don't argue!' shouted Dikran and went out.

Piloun stood where she was, astounded; the broom fell from her hand; her eyes moistened and she dried her tears with a corner of her apron; she went to the neighbour's small boy and asked him to take the bracelet to Khambourents Hadji Agha.

When Memik Hatoun opened the door, the small boy handed her the bracelet wrapped up in some paper and said:

'Dikran-the-Goldsmith's wife sent this.'

Memik Hatoun exclaimed:

'Oh my, oh my...!'

The boy flew away. Memik Hatoun did not open the parcel, but took it straight upstairs, put it in front of Hadji Agha and said:

'See how shameless she is: she has sent you a present!'

'Who has, wife?'

'Your sweetheart!'

Hadji Agha was shaken. There was a silence.

The parcel remained between the two of them and neither would open it.

'Has your tongue dried up?' rudely screamed Memik Hatoun.

Hadji Agha said in a gentle voice:

'Tell me, Memik, what is this? Who is mad, you or I, or is it the world?'

'It's you!'

'Ah well, it's a good thing that I am the only one who has gone mad, that the world is sane, and that you are sane!'

There was a quavering in Hadji Agha's voice, which made Memik Hatoun feel sorry for him; her eyes were filled with tears and she embraced her husband and, with a caressing voice, said:

'Hadji Agha, tell me, for the love of God, are all these things lies?'

'They are, Memik, they are lies! If they are not, may I not rise from my bed in the morning and may I be carried out of the house in a coffin!'

Memik Hatoun seemed to have believed him, but the parcel had to be opened, and they did: only to find the bracelet in it!

Hadji Agha and Memik Hatoun, astonished and almost demented, looked at each other: a bracelet!

'Blessed be the Lord...!' whispered Hadji Agha.

Memik Hatoun pondered for a long time and, having reached a conclusion according to appearances, she exclaimed:

'Well, Hadji Agha...?'

'Don't ask any more questions, Memik! You said a little earlier that I had gone mad; you were right, I have gone mad!'

'Oh my, what is this: does a man send a woman a bracelet, or does a woman send one to a man?'

'As the world has become topsy-turvy, Memik, it makes no difference, you can have it that way also,' replied Hadji Agha, but in the light of his eyes could already be seen the impending signs of real insanity.

Memik Hatoun whispered to herself, in a way to let Hadji Agha hear her:

'Just look at that stuck-up wench, she didn't like it and sent it back!'

Hadji Agha swung round as if he had been stung, he looked at his wife and asked:

'Is that what you think?'

'What else can I think?'

Suddenly Hadji Agha shouted in a loud voice the like of which Memik Hatoun had not heard in all her married days with him.

'You are the mad one! The world is mad! Get out, out, out!'

Memik Hatoun, frightened of his anger, left the room and she had barely climbed down two steps when she sat on the stairs, sensing that she was losing her balance. Fortunately, her daughter arrived just then and she told her the story of the bracelet. The daughter was also convinced of the conclusion her mother had reached: that it was her father who had sent the bracelet to Dikran-the-Goldsmith's wife, that she had not liked it and had sent it back in her annoyance.

Memik Hatoun's crying did not cease, in spite of her daughter taking her downstairs almost in her arms, washing her face and endeavouring to console her with the tenderest words.

'What black snow is this that has sifted on to my head...?' Memik Hatoun kept saying and beating her knees.

The daughter, seeing that her mother would not be pacified, suggested taking her to her own home for a few days.

'Come and stay with us for a few days and we'll see what happens,' she said.

'What can happen? It'll be Sodom and Gomorrah all over again, and we will be burnt up in it,' replied the mother and, pulling her shawl on to her head, she followed her daughter.

When Memik Hatoun told her son-in-law all about the incident, he declared with determination:

'It's all lies; I don't believe any of it!'

The son-in-law had heard the slanderous rumours outside, and was only unaware of the bracelet incident, which seemed equally improbable to him.

'Well, son-in-law,' said Memik Hatoun, 'the boy who brought it said that Piloun had told him to give her greetings to Hadji Agha and to tell him that it was she that had sent the bracelet to him!'

'There is something funny in all this; be a little patient and we'll see what'll come of it,' concluded the son-in-law, and he was prepared to go and clear the matter up with his father-in-law, but neither his wife nor her mother would let him.

Hadji Agha was alone in the house and did not sleep a wink that night; he did not even take off his clothes, and spent his time meditating. It did not occur to him in the least that his wife was not at home, and he thought that she must be sleeping in the other room, not wanting to see his face.

The whole night, in the silence and the solitude, a thousand and one thoughts passed through his mind, but he was unable to reach any conclusion: every now and then he would be firmly convinced that he had lost his sanity, but every time he came to that decision, a slight smile would involuntarily appear on his face and he would mutter to himself: 'Very well, if I have gone mad, I have! But does a madman himself know that he has gone mad?'

After midnight, he heard sounds in the house once or twice. He went to the door, listened and, meeting the dense walls of silence, he returned to his corner, where he sat and, smoking

ceaselessly, he thought. Towards morning, he suddenly decided
to go to Dikran-the-Goldsmith, to have a talk with him and clear
everything up. When he had taken this decision, he felt lighter
both in mind and in body—in his body which seemed to have
grown as heavy as a corpse.

The following morning was Sunday; Dikran would be at home,
and he could go and see him there, and where he could even speak
in the presence of Dikran's wife and so clear up all misunder-
standings.

He waited a long time for Memik to come in; but she did not
appear, and he decided to go, as there was no point in waiting any
longer. Memik must have gone to church, he thought to himself,
and, putting the bracelet in his pocket, he went below. The house
was completely silent; he went into the kitchen, but there was
no one there. When he was about to open the front door, he
stopped there: should he go or not; what was he to say if he did
go; where was he to begin; what was there that he should begin
with at all? Then, he decided to begin with the bracelet and he
stepped out with determination.

He would not look at anyone in the street, in order to escape
from irritating looks. Those who saw him up to Mehmet Pasha
Gardens did not pay much attention to him, they thought he was
on his way to church. But when from there he turned into
Boshayents Street, there was not one inattentive look left; a few
people even went back to see why he had turned into Boshayents
Street. Hadji Agha went and stood in front of Dikran-the-
Goldsmith's door and, without hesitation, he knocked on it and
waited. If anybody had looked at him at close quarters, he would
have seen a film of sweat on his forehead and he would have
noticed that he was shaking like a leaf in his whole body. His head
was bowed and he was looking at the ground, without raising his
eyes.

Had he raised his eyes, he would have seen standing in the
distance twenty-five to thirty people, who were impatiently waiting to find out what would happen; he would have seen Elmass
Hatoun and the other daughters-in-law, who were watching him
from the window opposite almost leaning on one another. They
were waiting for Piloun to open the door, invite Hadji Agha inside
and throw her arms round his neck, so that they might witness
it all a second time.

Suddenly Piloun appeared at the balcony and called out:

'What did you want?'

'I want to see Mister Dikran.'

'He is not at home.'

'When will he be back?' asked Hadji Agha, but he could almost not see any more, because he had looked up and his eye had caught the women at the window opposite and the people standing in the street.

'I don't know!' replied Piloun and withdrew from the balcony, quivering.

Hadji Agha's footsteps mechanically turned back. He continued his way, with his head bowed, barely distinguishing the paving stones from the narrow stream which ran down the side of the street. He could hear exclamations which pierced his ear:

'When he saw that there were people about, he said: "I want to see Mister Dikran!" ' somebody called out, pulling faces.

'Piloun is calling you, Hadji Agha...!'

'Hadji Agha has had his fun...!'

Hadji Agha reached home, bathed in an icy sweat; he went inside, shut the door and sat there behind it, saying to himself: 'This is the sweat of death!'

Memik Hatoun did not put in an appearance. He gathered up his strength somehow, climbed to the room upstairs and, approaching the window, he looked out stealthily. There was no one in the street. Those who had followed him had dispersed; this reality invigorated him and he felt lighter. To stop the trembling of his body, he gulped down a few glasses of rakki; then he sat in the corner and began to think of a way out.

The more he thought, the more the whole world before his eyes darkened. What had started it all? What had happened? Why had that girl sent him a bracelet? Should he have thrown it up on to the balcony from below, so that they could all see his refusal of the present? Perhaps it was a mistake for him not to have done this; perhaps it was essential for him to go and hurl the bracelet up on to the balcony and return home again.

His thoughts were becoming increasingly searing: it seemed as if red-hot skewers were being thrust into his brain and pulled out again; as if a powerful and coarse hand had seized his heart and was squeezing it like a lump of meat. Suddenly, he stood up, went to the door and called down:

'Memik...!'

He called out and immediately stopped, because his voice

faltered and lost its natural tone; it seemed to him that an alien voice was calling his wife. He withdrew, went to the mirror and was barely able to recognize his face. He walked towards the corner of the room, but he began to sway in his whole body; and the whole room swayed also: the ceiling bent down and then straightened itself up again, the lamp hanging on the wall touched the carpet on the floor and went back to its place again. However much he tried to roll a cigarette, he did not succeed: he looked at his two fingers and saw an enormous space between them. At last he reached the corner of the room, flopped down, put his head to the pillow and shut his eyes.

When the service ended and Dikran-the-Goldsmith came out of the church, he too became subjected to a shower of strange looks.

He was still in the porch of the church when he heard:

'He has come to church! Huh, go home and see who's there!'

He heard this and, although he was not definitely convinced that it concerned him, he nevertheless turned round. He saw sarcastic smiles on people's faces. He was shaken. As he left the porch of the church, he heard someone say:

'Hadji Agha has gone to visit Piloun...!'

There was no room for doubt this time. It was only by instinct that Dikran-the-Goldsmith found his way home.

As soon as he entered the house, he shouted loudly with rage:

'Who was it that came here?'

Piloun looked at Dikran's eyes and she was terrified, and through her terror she forgot everything; she leant against the wall and with glassy eyes looked at the colourless expanse. Dikran went to her.

'Who had come to visit you?' he asked in a terrifying voice.

Piloun was unable to reply anything. Dikran dragged her by the shoulder and hurled her to the floor.

'Who came here, I ask you, and you won't open your mouth, eh...?' he shouted with his anger at its peak, and raising the pitcher of water he hurled it at her.

Once more instinctively and mechanically, Piloun evaded the blow. The pitcher struck the wall and shattered into smithereens with a loud crash.

'Dikran...!' the innocent woman barely managed to utter.

'Do you still dare mention my name, you shameless wench!' shouted Dikran and once more went to her.

No imploring look had any effect on the demented husband.

'You didn't come to church so that you could have fun with Hadji Agha, eh? I'll teach you how to have fun now!'

Piloun wanted to say that Hadji Agha had only come to see him, but Dikran did not let her, for he attacked her ferociously, seized her by the throat with both hands and began to squeeze. Piloun's eyes bulged and reddened; she clawed at Dikran's face with her nails, which made him even wilder, and he squeezed her throat with the greater force and greater physical power of a maniac. Suddenly Piloun went limp, her neck no longer offered any resistance, so that Dikran's fingers were thrust into his wife's flesh. And as if he held a mass of dough between his hands, her whole body lost its firmness and she collapsed on to Dikran's knees like a rag. He started instantly and was horrified; he let Piloun's body drop on to the floor and began to call out:

'She's dead! She's dead! She's dead...!'

His voice was so loud and so heart-rending that all the neighbours heard him and rushed to his front door. Dikran wanted to open it, but his knees were shaking and he was unable to take a single step. Those gathered in front of the door heard Dikran emitting sounds, which seemed like crying, but they were bestial sounds.

One or two of the young men there, seeing that Dikran would not open the door and sensing the presence of some horrible crime inside, walked round to the back of the house, climbed on to the wall and jumped down into the garden, went inside the house and opened the front door. The crowd rushed in. Piloun's body had collapsed lifeless on the floor. Dikran had retired to a corner, where he was down on his knees, with his head resting against the wall, and he was sobbing.

The news of the crime spread throughout the town quicker than lightning.

'Dikran-the-Goldsmith has strangled his wife!'

'Woe, Hadji Agha, woe...!'

Memik Hatoun, too, heard the news of the crime, while she was still in her daughter's house; she heard it in its every detail: Hadji Agha had called on Piloun while her husband was in church. She had received him inside; the goldsmith had heard about it on his way home and had demanded an explanation from his wife; she had remained silent, and...

3

'That man has gone off his head!' exclaimed Memik Hatoun and ran home.

Hadji Agha had not heard anything about the crime.

As soon as Memik Hatoun returned home, she beat her knees with her hands and cried out:

'Hadji Agha, Hadji Agha, all honour is lost, everything is lost...!'

Hadji Agha heard this cry but paid no attention to it, because he did not suspect anything new; he thought it was still the continuation of the same incident, but voices began to be heard from below the window: he heard his name mentioned, Piloun's name, the goldsmith's house mentioned. At first, Hadji Agha decided to keep calm. 'They will bark and bark and then go away,' he concluded to himself and rolled a cigarette; but the voices grew louder and more persistent.

'He's finished off his young, pretty wife!'

'What will his answer be on the Day of Judgement?'

'He visited the wife by broad daylight!'

Hadji Agha was unable to resist it: he went to the window.

There was a crowd of people in the street: they all had their eyes fixed on the window.

Hadji Agha drew back and began to listen: he could not tell what new incident had taken place from any of the exclamations, but a gloom settled upon his inner world. After listening to the voices for some time and failing to reach any conclusion, he drank down two more glasses of rakki and went downstairs, to find out something from Memik.

'Memik...!'

Memik Hatoun raised her head and, with terrified eyes, looked at her husband. First of all, his voice made her shudder; it was altogether an alien voice, it did not possess the familiarity of the past thirty-five years: and then, Hadji Agha's face had changed, it had become noticeably older and gloomy, his eyebrows hung down on to his eyes, like the eaves on to the blind windows of a house in ruins.

'Memik...!' once more voiced Hadji Agha.

'I wish Memik were buried in the ground and had not seen these things!' she replied.

Hadji Agha was silent; it seemed as if he could see through the thick walls the crowd in front of the house.

'What has happened, Memik, tell me?' he said.

She took pity on him; there was such a tone of supplication in his voice that even the most indifferent person would have been moved.

'For the love of God, Hadji Agha, why did you do these things?' uttered Memik Hatoun, crying.

'But what have I done, dear? What have I done...?'

Memik Hatoun told him all about the terrible incident...

'Did he strangle her?' asked Hadji Agha.

'Yes...he strangled her...'

Hadji Agha swayed a little; with one hand, he took hold of the banister of the staircase, he raised the other hand to his forehead to wipe away the cold sweat which had instantly appeared there, and slowly he climbed up to his room. As he did so, it seemed to him that he was moving towards an increasingly deeper darkness; the atmosphere seemed to grow black, become dense, and turn into tar. He even smiled as he entered his room, for he did not recognize it; his own room of many years had lost its outward appearance. Perhaps the voices from the street were audible, but not with the clarity of a little earlier, because Hadji Agha was plunged into an inextricable chaos. He found the cupboard almost by groping, he opened it instinctively and felt for the bottle of rakki like a blind man, he put it to his mouth and drank it down to the last drop. He was unable to put the bottle back in its place and released it in the air: it fell to the floor and was smashed. Memik Hatoun heard the noise and she whispered:

'He's smashing up the bottles, now! Smash them up and smash your head also, you shameless man!'

Suddenly an idea had lit up Hadji Agha's vision, like a small lighted match in darkness. The more this idea blossomed in his brain, the brighter his surroundings became: the objects assumed their former shapes, the room was lit up, the fragments of the smashed bottle became visible, one by one; he even smiled, whispered something, as if he were telling some secret to somebody; he turned his steps towards the door, left the room, went downstairs, entered the kitchen, opened the cupboard and brought out the washing-line, which Memik Hatoun had carefully coiled up; he put it under his coat to hide it from view, and again climbed up to his room. He seemed to be in a happy mood; he wanted to have a drink of rakki, but there was none left.

Memik Hatoun heard the table topple over with a crash, but she did not suspect anything, and again whispered:

'Shameless man!'

Then silence reigned in the house, as in a closed tomb.

The crowd in the street had not yet completely dispersed when Memik Hatoun decided to go upstairs to talk to her husband, spit in his face and demand that he did something to drive the crowd away.

By the time she entered the room, Hadji Agha had given up his soul: his body had grown longer and his feet almost touched the floor. When she saw his body stretched like a column to the ceiling, she emitted a horrifying scream and fell to the floor, barely able to call out a few times: 'Help...! Help...! Help...!'

The people in the street heard the scream and turned their heads up to the window with astonishment. Someone called out:

'Now he is strangling his wife!'

'Help there...!'

A few people went to the front door and forced it open. They all rushed inside and found Memik Hatoun fainted on the floor, while Hadji Agha's body stood erect like a pillar in the middle of the room.

Yeldiz

SUDDENLY, THERE WOULD be a rumbling in the street: horse-shoes would clatter on the flagstones, and the strident metallic sounds would ring out in the limpid air.

'It's Armenak! It's Armenak...!' everyone would cry out.

Not only the children, but people of all ages would pour out of the houses and the shops into the street; women and maidens would fly to the windows; even those lying ill in bed would beg to be taken closer to the windows.

From the side streets, people would run panting and would crowd down the length of both sides of the main street in the town.

'Hey, it's Armenak!' would be heard from various parts of the town.

The porters would put down their loads and would run grotesquely, with the humped supports on their backs for carrying goods giving them somewhat the appearance of camels. Whilst the owners of the loads would remain standing beside their belongings, waiting in despair for the porters to return.

People in the middle of a shave, with their faces fully lathered or half-shaved and a white towel on their chests, would fly up from their chairs and would run.

There would be a frenzied turmoil throughout the small provincial town. As the people ran about, they would trample and push and pull one another, in order to reach quickly the main street, where Armenak riding his horse would speed towards the newly-tilled, friable and slightly warmed, vast field.

Armenak was a tall, handsome youth; a lock of wavy hair cast a shadow on his forehead, and his fez was tilted back; he wore a dark-red, velvet waistcoat, with his shirt sleeves pushed up; his green, woollen-cloth trousers, which clung tightly to his body, displayed his shapely legs; he had an arresting moustache, full, red lips, a pointed chin, and sky-blue eyes arched with a pair of black eyebrows.

Armenak's father was a carpenter, a renowned craftsman; he would spare nothing for his one and only son; so that when the boy had enough of school and would no longer go there, Ousta Ovanness did not rebuke him:

'Let him be healthy, if he can't be educated! I didn't go to school either, but I became somebody,' he said.

Armenak, however, learnt his father's trade and turned into a master craftsman; but he would hardly ever work in the shop, for he was burnt up with a passion which was akin to madness.

This was his love for horses.

Every Friday, Armenak would run to Giul-Ovan, a large field, which was tilled and crumbly, where people would hold contests on horseback with arrows; and he would watch the running of the horses, and each one of the contestants would appear like a legendary hero to his eyes.

On summer mornings, he would go to the Lower Square, where the horse-dealers used to buy and sell horses.

'Where did you get to, my boy?' his father would ask.

'They sold a horse like a young girl for five pounds!' would reply Armenak, swallowing his spit.

He would even stop and watch some mangy horse being shod.

For Armenak, a horse was the main object in life.

Ousta Ovanness listened to his wife, Anna Korro, for a long time and did not buy a horse for Armenak, because she would cry and would plead with her husband, night and day, secretly from their son.

'Do whatever you like, but don't get him a horse!'

Anna Korro was convinced that a horse would make the boy forget his parents and his two sisters; and, furthermore, a mother's greatest dream—of having her son married and a pretty bride brought into the home—would not be realized.

Whilst the son, every time he saw his father alone and especially when the latter was in a good mood, would hang his head down and say:

'You haven't bought me a horse, father!'

'I will, my boy, I will!'

It was most upsetting for Ousta Ovanness to see his son looking so miserable, with his head hanging down.

'He is so young, poor boy!' he would think.

And one day, Ousta Ovanness had a dream, in which Armenak was riding a donkey, prodding and kicking its belly as if he were racing on a horse.

He got up in the middle of the night, made himself a cup of coffee, which he sipped, as he smoked and pondered.

Anna Korro also woke up.

'Why are you up, dear?'

'I had a dream.'

'May it bode well!'

And Ousta Ovanness told her his dream.

'No-o, my dear...?'

'Ye-es...!'

Anna Korro cried.

'Oh, my Armenak riding a donkey...?'

'I saw it with my own eyes, wife!'

In the morning, Ousta Ovanness embraced his son and said:

'Go and choose yourself a horse, and I'll buy it for you, my boy; go on, now!'

Armenak flew away to the Lower Square.

Anna Korro cried, but she did not protest any longer.

Armenak's two sisters fluttered about, because he embraced them both and hugged them so tightly as to hurt them, and he kissed them.

In three days, Armenak found a horse, and Ousta Ovanness counted eight Ottoman pounds into the dealer's palm.

Armenak was no longer to be seen in his father's workshop.

'Let him bounce about and enjoy himself, I have lots of apprentices to help me out,' said his father.

At that time Armenak was twenty-one.

The horse he had bought had a slight defect: it would strike its forefeet together. Armenak exchanged it for another horse by paying another two pounds.

One day, his father heard that Armenak had taken part in a contest; he did not reveal this to his wife, but she heard about it through her own acquaintances and she was filled with terror. In these contests, they would use real arrows and resort to a thousand and one hostile measures, even hitting people on the head and killing them. There was no responsibility for any deaths which occurred during these contests.

The mother called her son and taking his head, pressed it to her fragrant bosom and said:

'Don't go to these contests, my child, please; you could break my heart for ever!'

Armenak promised her not to take part in them any more.

Little by little Armenak achieved spectacular successes in the field
of horse-riding.

'Your son has turned into a horse-acrobat!' Ousta Ovanness's
friends would tell him.

'It must be in the blood,' would reply Ousta Ovanness, 'my elder
uncle was also mad on horses and knew how to handle them.'

The ones who rejoiced most at Armenak's passion for horses
were his sisters, whose innocent and naïve pride did not go
unnoticed in the town.

'I saw your brother on his horse, yesterday; he was just like a
king!' would say one of the sisters' friends.

'Where did you see him?'

'In the Upper Square!'

Both sisters would swell with pride like turkeys, to such an
extent that the friend would regret making the remark.

'There is not another like my brother; he is the only one in the
world!'

One year, Ousta Ovanness secured the contract for the wood-
work of a large government building and he earned a great deal
of money.

'Anna dear, let's get our Armenak married; I have made a lot of
money,' said Ousta Ovanness to his wife.

Anna Korro was unable to reply for joy.

'He must have had his fill of horses by now; let's get him tied up
with a girl; it'll bring him down to earth a little and he'll also
forget his horse,' continued Ousta Ovanness.

'Yes, yes, you are right!' Anna Korro clung on to her husband's
words.

A few days later, while Armenak was helping his father make a
delicate cabinet in the workshop, Ousta Ovanness told him the
tale of the aged father:

'Once upon a time, there was an old father; this father had an
only son; this son was mad about dogs and hunting, and he didn't
get married. The father called him one day and said, "My son, I
am going to die, but I am still looking over my shoulder, still
hoping. If you get married and have a child, I will not look over
my shoulder any more." The son said, "In that case, I will get
married." The old man blessed his son, who got married, had a
son, and the father died in peace.'

'What does this parable show?' asked Armenak, smiling innocently.

'It shows that your time to get married has come.'

'I want to go and see other countries first; I will get married when I return.'

Ousta Ovanness yielded once more to his son; he gave him a great deal of money and sent him to Adana, Aleppo, and Damascus.

As he saw him off, Ousta Ovanness kissed him and said:

'Now may good fortune go with you,
And may your path be level, too.'

The mother embraced his head, cried and said:

'I would give my soul for you, your mother's only son, so tall and big!'

The sisters kissed him and merely cried.

For the first time in his life, Armenak smoked in the presence of his parents.

When Ousta Ovanness returned home, he said:

'It really pleased me to see my Armenak smoke!'

'Oh, his sweet cigarette!' sobbed Anna Korro.

The day after Armenak's departure, Ousta Ovanness's house seemed in mourning; it was as if, tired after prolonged weeping, everyone was silent; even the objects in it were sad: a length of rope, which had been brought out of the cupboard for Armenak's journey and had not been needed, had sadly uncoiled itself and fallen in the passage.

On the third day, Anna Korro suddenly began to cry. The daughters ran into the room and saw that their mother had come across one of Armenak's handkerchiefs under the pillow.

'Don't fret, wife; let him have his fill of travelling also, and we'll do something about it!' would say Ousta Ovanness and would run to his workshop early in the morning.

While every evening, Ousta Ovanness and Anna Korro would sit and talk about Armenak.

'How many days is it since my Armenak has been gone, dear?' Ousta Ovanness would ask.

'Five days.'

'Today he'll get to...'

Ousta Ovanness would think for a long time and would mention the name of some place.

And it would be the same every day.

One evening, at the hour when daylight turns pink, Ousta Ovanness, sitting near the window, again asked:

'How many days is it since my Armenak has been gone?'

The elder daughter, Hadjikhass, replied:

'Twenty-eight days!'

'He will be in Adana today.'

He had hardly finished his sentence, when a horseman came and stopped in front of their door; he was wearing an Arab costume and riding a white horse.

Ousta Ovanness was almost tongue-tied and was barely able to utter:

'A letter has come from my Armenak!'

Hadjikhass ran to the window and cried out:

'O-o-oh! It's Armenak! It's my brother...!'

And indeed it was Armenak.

The white horse was neighing like a brass bell at break of day; it was rearing itself up and turning on its hind legs, like a young ballerina pirouetting.

Hadjikhass was the first to open the door, and she stood there transported; while her younger sister, Hazartert, shouted from a distance:

'Oh, my big brother...!'

'Bring a little sugar,' said Armenak to his elder sister.

Hadjikhass ran to fetch some.

At the door stood Ousta Ovanness and Anna Korro. Hadjikhass brought the sugar and timidly gave it to her brother. Armenak bent down on to the horse's neck and offered the sugar with his outstretched palm. After crunching this, the horse calmed down; whereupon, Armenak jumped down. His sisters threw their arms round his neck and he was hardly able to free himself in order to embrace his parents.

His mother cried.

Ousta Ovanness, unable to understand her tears shed for joy, became angry and said:

'Well now, wife, you cried when he left and you cry when he comes back!'

Armenak settled the horse in the stable and went upstairs.

His father asked:

'How did this happen?'

'I went to Aleppo, wandered about for a few days and saw this horse: I bought it with all the money I had, and I came back.'

'And you used to say that our son was not clever; do you see?'
Ousta Ovanness turned to his wife.

Anna Korro was astonished, because she had never said such a
thing.

Armenak had an Arab turban made of fine wool wound round
his head; he wore a light aba, a pair of voluminous trousers, and
on his feet he had a pair of red high-boots.

'Didn't you go to Damascus, boy?'

'No, I had no money left.'

'Did you spend it all on the horse?'

'It's a famous horse: the dam is English and the sire is Arab!
I wouldn't part with it for a hundred pounds!' declared Armenak.

'Well done, my boy!'

'What is it called?' asked Hadjikhass.

'Yeldiz!'

'Oo-ooh!' exclaimed Hazartert.

'I would give my soul for your Yeldiz, my son!' whispered
Anna Korro.

On the very day after, the news spread like lightning in the small
provincial town that Ousta Ovanness's son had brought back
from Aleppo a horse that used to belong to the son of the Khedive
of Egypt; and it was said that it would only eat sugar and raisins,
and nothing else.

A few days went by, and on the first Sunday that followed, just
as the mass had ended and all the people were pouring out of the
cathedral, Armenak brought Yeldiz out.

Its shrill neigh sounded through the peacefulness of a Sunday
morning, the astonishingly serene atmosphere.

'Fifty years ago, Moustapha Pasha had a horse like this one!
There hasn't been another like it!' they all said as they watched
Armenak, who, clinging tightly to Yeldiz's back, galloped
through the main street with the speed of a bird.

Ousta Ovanness's, Anna Korro's, and the two sisters' happiness
was boundless. On that Sunday morning many were the maidens
who said to their fiancés:

'Are you supposed to be a man? Look at Armenak, he is just
like a lion!'

Indeed, Armenak was that legendary youth, who, with his hair
tossing in the wind, soared in the air; he was that hero, who had
suddenly appeared, riding a fiery horse and had come to distribute

their cherished desires to all those who had suffered for their unattainable dreams.

'I would give my soul for your horse's shoe!' would whisper Armenak's mother, when she heard the ringing of Yeldiz's shoes as it burst on the white flagstones and scattered, like the golden cymbal of the sun upon the crests of the blue mountains and the tall, sombre trees of the forests.

That day hundreds of maidens fell in love with Armenak. One of them was even so daring as to approach his sister and whisper into her ear:

'If only I could lie with your brother once, they could come and bury me after that...!'

And on every Sunday and festive day, Armenak would bring out his horse, with a large turquoise stone hanging from its neck—to ward off evil eyes—and he would make the street rumble, with the horseshoes clattering on the flagstones and the strident metallic sounds ringing out in the limpid air.

'Armenak...! Armenak...!'

Yeldiz, white all over, with hoofs as black as coal, its noble head held high and proud, undoubtedly sensed that the whole town had come out to watch it race.

The day would turn into one of frenzy for the entire provincial town, a day of public rejoicing, a truly festive day.

That evening, all those who drank their wine—whether they knew him or not—would consider it their duty to drink to Armenak's and his horse's health.

'May they both live on and may they make our town shine!'

'Say what you like, the bastard's son deserves the horse. May God preserve him!'

That evening, in almost every home, the conversation centred around Armenak and his horse.

'Did you see him, dear...?'

'Of course, I did...!'

'I saw him as I was crossing the stream; my eyes were dazzled!'

'I was standing in the field, when I saw him coming like a fiery cloud...!'

And some would tell of such things which they had not seen, but which could have taken place. And the more things they had 'seen' the prouder they felt, and by repeating them over and over again, they themselves believed the stories they told.

'You know that tree on its own in the field, don't you? Well, he flew over that...!'

'No, really, my dear fellow!' would come the reply from someone, amazed and incredulous, but he would know well that the other was weaving fancies.

'A woman got in his way in the street, so Yeldiz flew over her and she didn't even know it!'

'You're telling me: it flew over my own head...!' a fourth would boast in all sincerity, fully convinced of it himself.

There were people, the worst idlers in the town, whose fezes were always tilted and who wandered about with only one arm thrust into the sleeve of their jackets—as a sign of insolence—the fabrications of these, even more colourful and legendary, they would relate to Armenak himself:

'Armenak, my dear fellow, you are up there, riding, and you can't see it yourself: you know Mardiros-the-Pauper's house at the other end of the street, don't you? Well, when you got there, Yeldiz curled itself up, put its hoofs on the roof, and away...!'

'Amazing!' would exclaim Armenak, with astonishment.

And in order not to 'pour icy water' over the horse's renown, and himself being a little transported, he would relate legendary tales:

'When I ride, a cloud seems to descend on my eyes, and I can't see anything!'

And they would all believe him, because they had firstly believed in their own lies.

There was one desire which consumed all the people in the town: it was to approach Yeldiz and stroke it, or at least to feel its breath from near.

However, that desire was not realized for any of them, for Yeldiz would refuse to allow anyone but Armenak to go near it. As soon as anybody tried, Yeldiz would become enraged, would neigh and rear itself up. Armenak himself made every effort to tame it towards the members of the family, but in vain; only on those days when Armenak was not home in time to give barley to the horse, would Hadjikhass go near, with the barley in one hand and some sugar in the other, and as she offered the sugar to the horse, she would pour the barley into the manger and would run.

'Very well then,' would say Ousta Ovanness, 'but how was it that it let you go near?'

'It took to me from the first day,' Armenak would reply.

'Animals can tell the difference in the human milk,' Anna Korro would conclude.

Months went by.

A year passed.

Two years passed.

Yeldiz's fame grew increasingly, the stories told around him became more and more colourful and numerous.

There appeared a group of ruffians in the town, who started looking for ways of stealing Yeldiz. This group was organized by a horse-lover who had come from another town. Having heard of Yeldiz's fame, he had stuffed his belt with money and had come to snatch Armenak's horse away.

'Who is that hooligan to have a horse better than mine!' had declared this ruffian.

He was joined by a few of the local youths whose fiancées, having fallen in love with Armenak, had spurned them.

Guessing the existence of this group, Armenak had transferred his mattress to the stable and would sleep there at night. On one side of the stable were the horse and the dung, and on the other side, a mattress with its bed-linen beautifully embroidered by Armenak's sisters.

When Armenak moved into the stable, Ousta Ovanness personally built double windows for it and covered them with iron bars, and he reinforced the door with heavy iron-bars; he even pulled down the roof, strengthened it with a double row of beams, which he covered up again.

'They can only steal my legs now!' said Ousta Ovanness when he had finished the work.

At last the time had come when Ousta Ovanness and Anna Korro had persuaded their only son to get married, but now this move into the stable had upset all their plans.

'Am I to take the girl to sleep in the stable?' protested Armenak.

Ousta Ovanness was unable to argue back, because he was firmly convinced that if Armenak did not sleep in the stable—with his revolver under his pillow and his unsheathed dagger next to the mattress—the ruffians would carry off the horse without fail, which would be tantamount to death for Armenak.

'It's better for my son to sleep in the stable and stay alive, dear,' he would persuade his wife, 'than to bring home a bride and die.'

'Let the bride sleep in the stable also!' would say Anna Korro.

'Wife, say something which will not make a cooked chicken laugh!'

One day, Armenak's mother innocently tried to persuade her son to sell his horse and lead a proper life.

'You have already had your fill of the horse!' she said.

Armenak replied:

'I wouldn't exchange one of my horse's hoofs for forty girls!'

The sisters favoured Armenak's celibacy: they were afraid that if a bride entered the home, she would appropriate their brother completely.

The more the parents spoke of marriage, the more Armenak's love for his horse deepened, and after each talk he would bring out the animal and make the street rumble.

In spite of her moistened eyes, when Anna Korro heard Yeldiz neigh, she would exclaim:

'I love the sound of your cry...!'

Yeldiz grew increasingly luxuriant and more enraged.

Armenak led a life of supreme happiness. The smell of the dung in the stable seemed most fragrant to him. Sometimes, he would rise in the middle of the night, would go to Yeldiz, caress it, and kiss its eyes, which would assume a boundless gleam and depth as they stared at the lantern; then he would go back to bed, smoke a cigarette, and go to sleep. It would happen that Armenak would be late going to bed; Yeldiz would become restless, and when he entered the stable the horse would let out such a neigh that the panes of the stable-windows would rattle.

But profound happiness does not last long. This seems to be the unintelligible law of nature: the abundant fall of rain is brief; when the fruits on trees grow large and succulent, they are small in number; likewise when the morn is flooded with light, suddenly clouds arrive, grey, dark and heavy clouds, and cover the infinite blue of the sky.

Armenak suddenly fell ill and began to cry out repeatedly:

'My stomach...! My stomach...!'

Immediately, they transferred him from the stable to the house, back to his former bedroom. They tried hot water, and hot bricks; the doctor came in the middle of the night: he gave some medicines and advised a compress; but nothing helped.

'It is strangulated hernia!' he announced.

And the doctor of this small provincial town, having pronounced Armenak's illness, folded up his arms and withdrew to one side. His knowledge was powerless to help.

Armenak did not cease to cry out.

The following night he barely managed to beg his father to go and spend the night in the stable.

'The ruffians may do something to my horse,' he said.

Ousta Ovanness spent that night in the stable.

In the morning Armenak's condition had deteriorated: his colour had completely changed, his heart pounded all the time; his intestine was knotted and he was in great discomfort.

Even in that dying state, Armenak did not forget his horse, and the following night somehow or other he managed to ask his father to go and sleep in the stable again.

Ousta Ovanness once more went to the stable; once more he verified that the revolver was under the pillow. Then, he lay down, but Yeldiz would not let him sleep, ceaselessly stamping the ground with a monotonous rhythm.

Ousta Ovanness stood up and went to the horse. Yeldiz did not display any rage that night, it only stamped the ground ceaselessly and obstinately. He gave it some sugar in his palm, but the horse would not eat it and continued to stamp.

Ousta Ovanness could not sleep, he sat up on the mattress, smoking and thinking. His thoughts were sad and sometimes grotesque. The night had brought him ill-omened visions.

Towards morning, when the little windows of the stable were still barely tinted with blue, the horse speeded up its stamping, which hardly lasted a few minutes more, and suddenly ceased: there was not another movement; the horse merely emitted a groan and hung its head down sadly and gloomily. Ousta Ovanness went to it, looked into its eyes: there was something human in its gaze; he stroked the animal's neck and head, freely and without fear. Yeldiz made no effort to move; it looked sadly at Armenak's father, only once. It was as if someone had stabbed Ousta Ovanness: an evil and terrifying thought pierced his brain like a dagger. He ran out.

He had to cross the very small garden to reach the house from the stable. He had hardly taken a few steps, when he heard his wife's and daughters' wailing. His legs gave way and he collapsed; he picked himself up and, swaying from side to side, holding on to the trees and bushes, he moved forward.

At that very moment the horse had ceased to stamp, Armenak had closed his eyes forever.

The whole district awoke from the weeping and lamenting, and they crowded into Ousta Ovanness's house.

When the long funeral procession stopped in front of the door and the coffin appeared in the street, Ousta Ovanness went to the stable, broke away Yeldiz's rein, and released it. With sad and slow, unsteady steps, like those of a human-mourner, the horse approached Armenak's coffin, touched the wood with its muzzle, and stood there.

The procession began to move. The further it went forward, the more it grew, until almost the whole town took part in the funeral. The horse walked in pace with the procession, never taking its muzzle away from Armenak's coffin.

In the cemetery, when they put down the coffin and placed it on the mound of earth dug up from the grave, Yeldiz hung its head down on to Armenak's face and people saw its tears, great big tears, hot and nostalgic, pour down on to Armenak's face.

'It is crying like a human being!' the mourners whispered.

'Oh, my brave lion, I would give my soul for your horse's shoe!' lamented the mother.

The sisters fainted and were carried to one side; while Ousta Ovanness held the horse's neck with one hand and Armenak's hand with the other, and lamented.

'Oh, my big, handsome boy, Yeldiz has become an orphan!' he said and mingled his tears with those of the noble animal.

When they lowered the coffin into the deep grave, Yeldiz put its muzzle on the edge of the grave and remained in that position, until the earth filled level with the ground and rose above it.

When the funeral procession began to move back, Yeldiz once more parted the crowd, approached Armenak's mother, bent down its head, put it under her arm, and kept it there all the way home.

During the whole of the return journey, Yeldiz walked sadly, with the sadness of a human.

The entire town wept for Armenak and the orphaned horse.

'The animal also seems to have a heart like a human being!' they said.

The Apricot Tree

IT IS MIDNIGHT.

It is one of those spring nights when concrete reality and violet dreams mingle together, for the fragrance which floats up from the newly-sprouted grass and the pink apple-blossom is like the fragrance of the rippling, diaphanous veils in a dream.

The bosom of the night is filled with murmurs.

It is the voice of flowers opening, the cry of sweet pain from tearing buds.

The buds are rending their hearts: the irresistible, ruthless and ardent desire of creation is death, inevitable and eternal death.

The cool air, in the blue streams of heaven, sparkling and trembling with starriness, flows upon earth and upon spring.

Beneath one of the roofs of the world, upon a marble table, under a green lamp-shade, a large book lies open. Over that book is inclined the scientist's head, which is tired and upon which the first universal snow has already settled. That head is tired, for it is infinitely difficult to unravel each knot in the book, difficult to understand the complex meaning of its sculpture, filled with wrath, with hatred, with light, and with love.

At midnight the scientist's eyelids close, like the mist which descends upon the little, blue mountain-lake.

And the brain ceases working.

And when the brain ceases working, the heart rejoices, for when the mind is tired, flutes burst into tune in the heart, flutes which evoke memories of the past.

And when the heart is awakened and the flutes sound, the folds of long ago in the heart are opened out.

Both innumerable and fragrant are those folds.

Even some distressing, poignant sorrow of old is fragrant, though still issuing smoke from one of the folds.

And from each fold a zephyr blows, spreading old but fresh fragrances around.

Now a breeze from the past in the late spring rises from one of the folds and sings in the green fields.

The brain is eternally renewed, discarding that which grows

old, like useless objects from a room; but the folds of the heart preserve, tenderly and unimpaired, all the sounds, all the colours and all the fragrances of long ago. The heart is strange: it remembers with sweetness and with bliss even the death which came one day of old, embraced and carried away the beloved-one, on the merciless understanding never to be returned.

The night sways on.

The mountains float in undulating waves; the trees flutter; the gardens flow with pregnant cheerfulness.

The earth has opened its heart and is pouring out its colours and forms; and the silence of the night itself is singing; the brooks are babbling and gurgling as they flow hurriedly on and on.

And the human heart flows on, rich with blood and warm.

With great longing and with tremulous warmth, yet another of the innumerable folds opens out.

Two leaves from an apricot tree have fallen there, still fresh and bright; under the leaves lies a lily-white hand, upon which fall the scientist's hot tears. The hand quivers from the warmth of the tears and revives. The leaves likewise tremble from the warmth of the tears and they grow: and now above his heart rises the whole apricot tree, resplendent in foliage and cooling freshness.

Out of the blue mist, like a lily out of the womb of the night, a maiden blossoms as beauteous as the sparkling Venus in the sky; she moves forward, treads upon the scientist's heart, and embraces the trunk of the apricot tree, with the embrace of an ivy, a flame, a beam of light. In her limpid eyes broadens the peaceful midsummer eve. The sun has already dipped behind the mountains, but in the foliage of the tree, the apricots light up like lanterns, as do the stars in the profundity of the sky. Which are the stars and which the apricots? They glitter as if they were fragments of the sun. The crests of the mountains have long grown dark; the sun's rays have left the blue waters of the little mountain-lake, now likewise grown dark: and out of its waves seems to have emerged a naked maiden, of lily radiance. The midsummer evening-breeze rustles and tosses her hair about, like a flame before a wind. Her hair is fragrant, as is the grass. The mother-of-pearl reflections from the moon are cast upon the grass, the sword-like leaves of the maize, and the bowl of the sunflower. The apricots are lit up in the moonlit night, and the maiden's eyes are glittering.

The whole universe is filled with fragrances.

This fold, out of the many in the scientist's heart, has turned into a complete existence, real, tangible, and present.

And the memory is set ablaze: the entire past is resuscitated and blossoms out anew.

That past is purified and cleansed, like gold from earth and base metals, it is purified from pain, from poignant grief.

He was a student in the capital of the empire and had gone there from the furthermost part of the realm. During the whole of the academic year he studied eagerly and with rapture, and he remembered with longing the old village; and when the year of study ended, he hurried back to the village by train.

And now he had alighted at the railway station of the little town. He had no desire to stop a single minute at the station; his eyes were longingly fixed upon the mountains of the village. The fragrance of the fields filled his nostrils even in the station. His childhood frisked about in the fields; it frisked about, drunk with the breeze and the fragrance of the grass.

The young student's heart and mind had both grown tempestuous; for him life was an untamed storm, with himself as a bird with golden wings.

From the distant regions of the open fields, his childhood came running as a personified being. This, his childhood, was as light as a breeze, green like an emerald, smiling like a dew on a rose-petal at break of day, prattling like the babble of a mountain spring. He walked through the tall grass in the fields, arm in arm with his childhood. The dew of dawn moistened his heels and his student's clothes, as if with children's tears. Overhead was the lapwing's humoresque; at his side, his childhood; underfoot, mother earth; in his heart, a young maiden with dimples in her cheeks; on his brow, the smile of the fields and the sunlight.

He opened out his arms anxious to embrace them all: the wind sang in his arms and blew past.

He reached home. The hens were scratching about in the ground in front of the house; the cock called out to his female partners, loudly and proudly; the hens scattered.

The mastiff jumped down from the flat roof and threw its arms round him. He kissed the dog with sincerity, warmth, and affection. The mastiff sniffed away at him and, drunk with his scent, exposed its white, pointed teeth and pink gums.

He went into the house, kissed his mother and his earth-scented grandmother, buried his head into their bosom.

They talked and questioned one another at length and in detail. Then he bathed, combed his hair, replaced his travelling clothes with his student's jacket, with its yellow and shiny buttons.

He ran out of the house as the evening was rising from the fields towards the mountains. A golden dust floated in the pink twilight air.

Was it a dream? No, a condensed reality.

A fair maiden, with a red pitcher at her shoulder, was returning from the fountain. The evening rays were entwined round her feet and her hair.

These pink rays touched her brow also.

He knew this fair maiden, as he knew all the other maidens, but she had danced with his childhood.

And he called out from the depth of his heart:

'Arevhat!'

Arevhat turned round.

Who was it that had called? Perhaps the voice had sounded in her heart.

But he was standing before her, dressed in his student's clothes, with its yellow and shiny buttons.

Arevhat was thin, a little pale, and a little sad. But her whole being was smiling; her smooth, pink arms, covered with a fine down, like that of a peach, were smiling; her hand was smiling.

Neither of them spoke, but they listened to the voices of each other's gaze. The young student looked at her brow and it seemed to him that the sun having set, had risen again at the crest of the mountain.

'Let me have the pitcher.'

'No, I can manage.'

The student took the pitcher from the maiden and they walked on together; Arevhat was playing with the plait of hair which had fallen across her bosom.

'When did you come?'

'Today—a little earlier.'

Arevhat smiled, tilting her head round. The evening brightened in the student's soul.

They approached her house. Arevhat took the pitcher back and flew inside; she put it in the corner. She felt her heart with her hand: it was palpitating.

'What happened to the water, Arevhat?'

'It is here, *nanni*.'

Arevhat's voice trembled.

'What is the matter, daughter?'

The following morning, they met again; in their silence, they heard the throbbing of their hearts.

They met again and they were silent again.

The holidays went by and the student disappeared from the village horizon. A sweet sorrow remained from it in Arevhat's soul: an unquenched thirst and a boundless, a fearful yearning.

'What has happened to you?' asked her mother.

'Nothing, *nanni*,' replied Arevhat, restraining her tears.

And autumn came, golden and chill; winter came, white and melancholy; and then spring opened out: the streams sang under the ice, the grass smiled from under the ice, the ice thawed, the apple tree blossomed, and so, too, blossomed the apricot tree.

'He is here! He is here!' called out the village maidens.

Instinctively Arevhat, with the instinct of a maiden in love, sensed that it was he. She pressed her hand to her bosom, but her heart flew out and she flew up to the roof-top, in the wake of her soaring heart. She hid behind the thick growth of ivy. There was an unbounded restlessness within her soul, which brought a happiness to the young maiden. Her arms were empty: she wanted them to be filled.

'Arevhat! Daughter...!'

It was her mother's sad voice again, monotonous and merciless.

Arevhat's attention was focused towards the fountain, which gurgled out of a crevice in the dark-blue rock at the end of the village.

'Daughter...!'

Arevhat opened a slit in the thick ivy growth and looked towards the village fountain, towards the street which led to it and the path which formed the continuation of this street.

'Daughter...!'

Arevhat did not hear anything, she was watching with yearning, barely holding back her heart. There he was, standing at the end of the path, dressed in his student's jacket!

The sun was at the crest of the mountain, exuberantly golden and large. His buttons shone, as did his brow, and the breeze of twilight ruffled his hair.

The herd descended from the mountains; the lowing filled the silence of the village. Her mother went to meet 'Maro' and took it to the stable.

Arevhat slipped out of the house. She met the student in the haze of dust raised by the herd, near the fountain. He held her arm; Arevhat tenderly drew it away: it was not dark yet and there were piercing eyes about; but the sun became bloodshot, sank behind the mountains; evening rose with blue wings from the valley, crossed the whole extent of the endless fields, enveloped the village, and ascended the mountains.

The blue wings of night came down, grew deeper and then black.

Arevhat was filled with trembling.

'Daughter...!'

You call in vain, *nanni*: you call in vain for the wind to return; in vain do you counsel the flower not to open when spring has come; in vain do you seek to fetter the heart that it may not pound, when the blood overflows and inundates the river banks of the body.

He took Arevhat's hand. They climbed up through the tall grass, the sunflower-plants, the dog-rose, the hawthorn, and other bushes, and they came to rest on the side of the mountain, under an apricot tree.

The tree rustled; the flame-coloured moon rose, turned white and began to swim in the blue, calm sea.

A lyre has suspended itself from a bough of the apricot tree and is trilling away. Is it a nocturnal bird warbling, or is it Arevhat's heart calling? It is the blood singing, the lyre of the blood that is hanging from the apricot tree. The cool night warms the heart, as does a draught of cold wine, the body. The hearts grow closer to each other, the emptiness of the student's arms is filled, and the downy hair on his chest is burning.

'My uncle is in the vineyard; he is guiding the water from the stream towards the cornfield,' Arevhat whispers with a maiden's cautiousness.

The young man does not hear anything. The apricot tree rustles, the stream sings, Arevhat's heart sings; the scent of her flowery dress has inebriated the very last drop of the young student's blood; his brain is on fire, his whole existence is ablaze. Who can oppose the flow of an intoxicated and flaming blood?

But Arevhat flies away from his arms; she runs, goes near the stream and listens: the distant, muffled sound of a spade being thrust into the earth can be heard. Arevhat's uncle is going up-stream, towards the depth of the vineyard. It is dark there under the trees. Arevhat returns, treading cautiously and gently, like a roe in a forest, and fills the emptiness of the student's arms, as the evening-dew fills the world.

'You are beautiful, Arevhat, warm and fragrant!'

And Arevhat enters deeper into his heart. He touches her cheeks with his fingers. She listens to the sound of the earth and of her blood. Her bosom swells like a white sail at sea. The apricots hang above their heads. The sun has lit them like lanterns, as if to leave behind large drops of its immense fires.

'Your hair is fragrant, Arevhat, it is fragrant like the grass; your breast is radiant, Arevhat, like the milky rock of the moon; your heart is singing, Arevhat, like the golden brook in the sky.'

A cloud veils the moon.

The shadow of the tree darkens.

Arevhat trembles; she trembles from the warmth; she snuggles more and more into the young man's strong arms; and the soft silken darkness envelops them both.

And they both listen to the voice of the earth:

'Sing with your blood; let the fountains of your hearts babble: I am the earth, cool me with your blood!'

They embrace each other like two flames, red and burning, two fires torn away from the sun.

And Arevhat's tears of happiness fall on to the grass and the earth.

And from her tears the grass cools, as does the earth.

And the lyre hanging from the bough crumbles.

The moon comes out from under the cloud.

The darkness thins, the night turns into an infinite veil woven with blue and silver threads.

Footsteps, heavy and muffled, go past the two sides of the vineyard. The passer-by's spade shines under the moon's rays, and under the moon's rays his forehead is sombre. So also are his eyebrows dark.

At home, the mother is calling with an anxious heart:

'Daughter! Daughter...!'

Silence.

She enters the room, feels Arevhat's bed with her hands: she is not there.

The mother does not know that her bed is the grass, green and velvety.

'Daughter! Daughter...!'

Stony silence.

Her maternal soul is troubled.

She goes up to the roof; she looks at the moon: it seems to her that the moon is her husband's, Arevhat's father's skull, which is roaming in the sky, restless and tortured; he is looking at the night, searching out his executioner. It seems to the poor, widowed woman that the wandering skull is rebuking her for failing to find his body and burying it, to give him eternal rest.

'Daughter! Daughter...!'

The night-breeze is playing in Arevhat's hair, *nanni*; her heart is singing as the lyre of nature; go, sleep peacefully, without fretting: your daughter is growing, like the poplar on the river bank; her blood is overflowing, like the river in the spring.

'Oho...!' Arevhat's uncle calls out from the edge of the vineyard.

The moon swims, like a restless skull that has found no grave.

The uncle shakes his head and, with the spade at his shoulder, he walks along the bank of the stream.

The mother comes down from the roof with tears in her eyes.

'Daughter! Daughter...!'

'I am here, *nanni*!' Arevhat calls out from her bed.

Her mother goes into the bedroom, approaches the bed, puts her hand to Arevhat's brow: the young maiden's forehead is burning.

'Where have you been, daughter?'

Arevhat wants to keep everything inside her heart, but a wave rising from her heart chokes her. She must tell everything; she must transfer her secret to her mother's heart. Let her mother's heart rejoice and be tormented.

'Darling *nanni*,' begins Arevhat, 'he is handsome, young, and strong; his shiny, yellow buttons are like daisies; his forehead is high and wise; *nanni* darling, I love him, just as you loved father.'

'This is shameful, daughter!'

'Shameful? Why, *nanni* darling?'

The mother kisses Arevhat, to wipe away the shame from her face, which is rosy, and, taking her by the hand, she pulls her out of bed and takes her to the window and shows her the moon.

'That is your father's head, roaming about in the sky, looking for a grave.'

'It is your love, *nanni*, that is restless; it is your heart, *nanni* darling, that wanders about in the valleys, in the fields, and in the sky, looking for his love.'

It is past midnight, and under the pale rays that fall inside through the window, mother and daughter shed handfuls of tears: the one, for her lost love; the other, for her newly-dawned one.

This time Arevhat accompanied him to the railway station of the little town. The golden, heavy ears of corn in the fields came up to Arevhat's bosom. The chill breeze was sad; the bowed willow-trees on the banks of the stream were sad; and Arevhat's heart was sad, but her eyes were smiling, like the sunbeams spread over the fields.

The student took hold of her hand. They were both trembling, like the ears of corn.

'I will be back; this is my last year, Arevhat, I will be back and you will become my wife.'

When she heard this, the young maiden closed her eyes in order to open them in her inner world and to listen for ever to that song which myriads of birds sing in the heart.

They reached the station.

The bell sounded.

It seemed to Arevhat that it was the church-clapper, instructing the funeral procession to advance towards the graveyard. The large, limpid tears roll down her cheeks; the soul is saddened, as if on the brink of death's pit; the song of the myriads of birds ceases.

A flowery handkerchief flutters from one of the windows of the train: it seems to her that it is the flame of her burning heart.

The train moves, and Arevhat, too, moves in the same direction; suddenly she is intercepted by an iron barrier; she leans against the bars and fixes her eyes on the flame of her burning fire, which gradually disappears as the train enters the forested gorge. She hears the muted bellowing down the valley.

The railway station of the little town empties: there is only a maiden, with dimples in her cheeks, with sad and tearful eyes, still looking at the rails which grow closer together as they recede and disappear into the horrible gorge.

The twilight ascends: gold and roses pour down on to the distant village; Arevhat walks through the cornfields, her head bowed down and her eyes filled with tears.

'Daughter! Arevhat...!'

'I am here, *nanni*.'

'What is the matter, daughter?'

'He has gone away, *nanni*.'

She nestles to her mother's heart.

No one can feel the anguish of a young maiden's love as much as her mother, who has given birth to her with love.

'I would die for your luminous face, Arevhat; I would die for your tender years!'

'The world is dark, *nanni*.'

'The world is bright, my only one; it is our hearts that are dark.'

They embrace each other, mother and daughter, and they cry, trying with their luminous tears to dissipate the darkness in their hearts.

But the darkness grew increasingly deeper, for the 'peace' of the world was disturbed: the workmen in their multitudes of millions were called up. Their masters drove them to bloody and terrifying war.

They also dragged the student away from his desk and drove him to the battlefront.

He recalled Arevhat:

'I will return when the snow of the apricot tree falls upon the ground and the breeze of late spring lisps in the fields,' he had said.

And when the snow of the apricot tree fell upon the ground and the breeze of late spring lisped in the fields, Arevhat ran to the railway station of the little provincial town and waited for him.

At the station, she was enveloped in misgivings, dark and uncertain, the misgivings of a maiden in love and aflame. Those misgivings were sifted from all the surrounding objects and immersed into her soul.

Her heart flew out when from the distant depth of the forested, dark gorge the train-whistle howled. Arevhat's arms were empty and hot, and they waited to be filled: but the train came and went; it brought noisy bustling crowds, poured out provisions unprecedented for the little provincial town, and it departed, carrying away other crowds and other provisions.

Other trains came, and they went away; but Arevhat's heart, huddled up and sad, remained in the long, black shadows of the poplars of the railway station.

'What happened, daughter?' her mother asked, anxious of

heart, when with tearful eyes, gloomy and head bent down, Arevhat returned from the railway station.

'He did not come, *nanni*,' replied Arevhat, and her heart crumbled like a gleaming dome in an earthquake.

Her tears were sombre and abundant, like the turbid torrents of spring running down from the mountains into the fields.

'He has deceived you, daughter!'

'No, *nanni*, no!'

'What has happened then, daughter?'

'It is the war, *nanni*!'

The mother had not envisaged the war: it had not yet reached their village with any of its consequences; but a few months later, they took away Arevhat's uncle also.

The mother cried after her only brother and felt that the battle-front was gradually nearing their peaceful and patriarchal village. Sugar became scarce, as did paraffin; black bread took the place of white bread; and with the arrival of every mail, heart-rending outbursts of tears would arise from several homes in the village, for the military authorities had informed them that 'on a certain day of the month, during an attack on certain heights, a certain young man of a certain village was heroically killed for his country'.

Arevhat would stand at the window of her upstairs room and shed silent tears with the arrival of each sad news from the front.

'Why are you crying, daughter?' her mother would ask.

'All the young men are being killed, *nanni*,' Arevhat would reply and shed floods of tears upon her mother's bosom.

And there were almost no men left in the village with the exception of those bowed with age; they all went to the battle-front: the war flared up more and more; the ferocity grew more intense, the human ferocity, which has neither size nor limit.

The war ended, but the student did not return home; he did not part with his rifle and the hand-grenades hanging from his side. At present, instead of his student's uniform, he was dressed in a grey great-coat, with a fur-cap on his head, and torn boots on his feet. His eyes shone with hatred and with the rays of the great morning. He entered the capital of the empire, together with the troops in revolt, and took part in the siege of fortresses and palaces.

Under the smoke and noise of hand-grenades, under the terrifying thunder of bursts from guns, his chest resting against a smooth paving stone of a street in the capital, he would release his bullets against the old world and he would recall, with warmth and with frenzied endearment, Arevhat, who was waiting for him, full of faith and full of love, in the ancient and peaceful village. The civil war would also end now and he would return to the station of the little provincial town, and there would be waiting for him, full of vigour and fresh beauty, Arevhat and his childhood; and through the fields, all the way to the village, he would frisk about with Arevhat and his childhood; he would bare his chest to the light of dawn and the maddening fragrance of the grass; they would reach the village, and he would climb up the side of the mountain with Arevhat; under the apricot tree, the purple of the sun would envelop them; the breeze would sing from the fields; everything would sing, even the decayed stone of the apricot, now fallen to the ground, would sing.

The student started from his reverie, for the guns roared: the old order was defending with a final exertion the forts and palaces which it had dominated for three hundred years, in order that it might not now abandon its thrones and its gold plates; but the halls of porphyry were already beginning to shake under the tread of heavy feet, and the debauchery of centuries gave way to the creative noises of the new world.

At midnight, the student, wearing his grey great-coat, weary and cold, began to dream once more: there he is, walking; a heated heart, and there the blood babbles and flows into the pink rivulets of the body, as if they were the purple torrents from the sun tumbling down the waterfalls of the body.

'Arevhat...!'

He cannot hear the sombre echo of his voice, which is reflected by the black walls of death, for the guns are roaring, the rifles are whistling, and the terrifying noise of the collapse of the old world dominates.

The north wind howls, the denuded trees rumble before the iciness, the telegraph-wires screech, but the Red partisan's heart is aflame with the fire of dreams: the dream of that new world, for the creation of which he has embraced the instrument of death; the dream of that maiden, who will meet him at the railway station of the little provincial town; the dream of that maiden, whose hot tears fell on to the grass and the earth, drop by drop; the dream of that distant maiden, whose love he will drink from the heart, pitcher by pitcher, and perhaps the five-pointed star will light upon the bosom of that distant land also, like his kiss upon her brow.

The civil war was set ablaze in Arevhat's sunny land, too. The rifles whistled on the heights of the patriarchal village. All the peasants, who were without clothes and whose bodies were scorched beneath the lashes of whips, had risen.

And one night, the whole village was awakened: the guns were roaring behind the mountains.

'They're here! The Whites are here!' rose the cry from every corner of the village.

There was panic.

At twilight the Whites occupied the railway station of the little provincial town and filled the fields. The peasants in revolt retreated from the village and moved towards new positions on the mountain-chain to the north, while the Whites advanced towards the village. The inhabitants also climbed up the mountains, behind the rebels. Arevhat called out:

'*Nanni*, oh, *nanni*, they have all gone and we are left behind!'

'Go into the stable, daughter,' echoed her mother in a half-demented state.

Arevhat and her mother had been unable to flee and were left in the village.

Arevhat went into the stable and embraced 'Maro'. The latter bellowed in a heart-rending tone.

The sound of heavy footsteps and the neighing of horses were heard from outside, while the rifles whistled from the mountain-chain to the north of the village.

The Whites, enraged and grown grotesque, seized the old women left behind.

'Where are the young girls of the village?'

'There are no young girls here; they all ran away,' replied a few of the old women.

But they slapped the old women in the face and demanded young girls. One of the women, in order to save her own young daughter, betrayed Arevhat.

And the Whites entered her home and searched everywhere. It was after midnight when they found Arevhat huddled against 'Maro'.

She screamed and called out in a heart-rending voice:

'*Nanni! Nanni…!*'

There was not a sound: one of the soldiers had already put a rough hand across her mother's mouth.

In the petrified darkness, the blood of innocence trickled drop by drop; teeth gnashed with frenzy; all the stars in the sky turned into shooting-stars and flew away from the canopy of heaven, and the world became dark.

In the morning, when the sun rose from behind the mountains, its white rays became soaked in blood, and flushed.

The White detachments moved on towards the chain of mountains.

The mother ran to the stable, she took into her arms Arevhat's inanimate, disfigured, white body, and she bewailed with frenzied shrieks.

'I would die for your luminous face; I would die for your tender years!'

And the mother heard the dead body reply:

'The world is dark, *nanni*.'

The blue and limpid canopy of heaven crumbled upon Arevhat's lilies; her mother's heart was rent and her motherly blood flowed in torrents.

The wind was wailing in the dark forests of pine-trees on the slopes of the mountains; each needle-shaped leaf seemed to be shedding sombre tears; the tall grass in the fields was swaying to and fro with heavy rhythm; for death, emerging from the dark valleys, roaming in the steppes, trampling and destroying vast and rich gardens, had come and was screeching horribly in the fields.

But in the spring, the apricot tree blossomed, fragrant and white; the blossoms were impregnated, and in the summer they were lit up as lanterns of the sun; the brooks babbled down the hills, while the bosom of the fields began to fill with stars when at the beginning of autumn the globules of grapes glittered.

The train entered the old and dark gorge, whistled shrilly, but its echo returned as a horrifying roar. And now, emerging from the gorge, it slithered through the green fields and came to rest at the station of the little provincial town.

It is evening: on the face of the station shines a red, five-pointed star. The Red partisan smiles and alights from the train. Almost everything has changed. Every time he had come to this station in the past he would have with him his student's case and his books, and he would be wearing his student's uniform with the yellow and shiny buttons; now he was wearing a grey great-coat and at his shoulder he carried a kit-bag, in which there was a piece of black bread and a few lumps of sugar, a tea-mug, and nothing else.

No one recognizes him. He looks in every direction anxiously and with palpitating heart: he is looking for Arevhat. He had written to say that he was coming home: why was she not there? Was it possible that time had changed her heart? The Red partisan is surrounded with misgivings, dark and wet. His steps turn towards the village where shone Arevhat's eyes. There is not a sound in the fields: only the grass is whispering softly; the flowers are fragrant, as before; there are stars in the sky: there seem to be more of them than before, perhaps they are Arevhat's tears which are suspended from the canopy of heaven.

As he approaches the village, the distressing lament of some affliction reaches his ear. It is the bewailing of a woman: without doubt, that of a mother. The sound is coming from the fountain. He goes towards it. The fountain gurgles as before: its song is monotonous and eternal. Near it, there is a woman sitting on a stone; her hair is dishevelled, her face distorted; she is crying and lamenting. The Red partisan approaches the demented woman: his heart flies out of its cage, his knees tremble, and his eyes darken.

'*Nanni!*' he barely utters.

And when his eyesight is restored, he sees Arevhat's mother running towards the mountains, like one possessed; she is fleeing from people.

In the daytime, she does not come down from the mountains, in order not to see people's faces; and at midnight, when the very last breathing creature has retired under cover, she descends to the village, sits at the head of the fountain and laments.

The Red partisan walked through the village; he knocked on Arevhat's door: some strangers opened it.

'What did you want?'

'Arevhat.'

'Arevhat is no more: they violated and killed her; her mother is alive, but insane...!'

And the student felt the darkness, the wetness, the coldness of the gloom which plunged into his soul.

The night became as black as pitch and turned to stone.

In the morning he climbed up the side of the mountain; he

embraced the trunk of the apricot tree, kissed the tree as if it were Arevhat herself; he kissed the earth where Arevhat's tears had fallen and, without returning to the village, he walked through the fields towards the railway station of the little provincial town.

The train once more entered the gorge, the Red partisan heard the thundering echo. It was the first time that no one was seeing him off; he looked towards the station and he did not see any flaming handkerchiefs for him.

He went and never returned again. The fighting had ended; the era of peace and of the creation of a new history had begun. The Red partisan again returned to his student's desk and began to peruse history with a new vision, but he did not part with his rifle of the civil war: he cleaned and polished it, and hung it above his head. He looked upon it not as an instrument of death, but one which, with united understanding, had created the new world and would strengthen it.

The fold of the heart closed up.

Silver was pouring down from the lamp-shade on to the marble table and on to that book which had revolutionized the century and had changed the course of the world.

The scent of Arevhat's flowery dress still dwelt in the scientist's nostrils. In the closed fold of his heart there remained anew two leaves from the apricot tree, unfaded and bright, and a hand as white as a lily.

The scientist stood up and went to the balcony.

It was a starry night.

Far, far away, beyond myriads of blue mountains and green fields, there stands the apricot tree. From its bosom hang the sun-hued apricots, like the stars in the canopy of heaven.

Far, far away, through myriads of blue mountains and green fields, there flow and babble away the streams, there pulses and rings the human heart, filled with blood and with warmth.

And a golden voice trills in the heights of the morning.

Who is it? Arevhat? No.

It is the skylark singing in the dew of morn.

The Two Graves

WE HAD A distant relative whom we used to call Uncle Avedis, or rather 'Avedis Amoudja', in the dialect of those parts. We were not the only ones to call him by this name, the whole town did—even the Turks.

To this day, however, I do not know exactly how he was related to us.

Avedis Amoudja and Kouvar Korro had been married for over forty years. They had neither chosen each other nor had they met before they were married: it had all been arranged by the parents, according to the custom in the old, vanished country.

They had lived together without arguments and quarrels for only a year or two after their marriage; for the remaining years, every single day some slight cause had occurred to lead to an argument, which developed into a quarrel.

'What's this, wife, the chickens have come into the room again!' would roar Avedis Amoudja, without making any attempt to drive them out himself, but would call his wife that she might do so.

'You've only got to say "Shoo!" and they'll go away, man!' Kouvar Korro would reply angrily and would herself call out:

'Shoo! Shoo! Shoo...! Shoo...!'

Avedis Amoudja would counter with:

'I'm not a chicken-chaser!'

'If you are not a chicken-chaser, what are you then?'

'I am a man! I am the one who wears the fez!' would declare Avedis Amoudja.

At first, Kouvar Korro would end the squabble there.

But, little by little, she came to the conclusion that the one who wore a fez on his head was both capable and duty-bound to chase away the chickens. And when Avedis Amoudja ordered her to drive them out, she would reply:

'You chase them out yourself! It wouldn't hurt your mouth!'

'Wife!' would roar Avedis Amoudja, threateningly.

'Don't keep growling so much!'

'Wife!' he would roar more loudly and coarsely.

'Don't shout at me, you lout!'

'Wife, I tell you!'

'Go and bawl at someone else!'

And at night when they went to bed, their breaths would not mingle, being annoyed with each other they would sleep back to back.

In the morning, without exchanging any words with his wife, Avedis Amoudja would go to the market, open up his tinsmith's shop and work until evening, without going home for lunch.

While Kouvar Korro would warm the meal a few times, thinking that he would turn up any minute to gobble it up; but in the end, realizing that his anger could not have subsided yet, she would put the meal away in the cupboard and go to her neighbour to grumble.

'Avedis Amoudja (Kouvar Korro used also to call him Amoudja)—Avedis Amoudja is sulking like a child and hasn't come home for lunch.'

'Don't take any notice, all men are like that. He'll come slinking back in the evening!' the woman next door would encourage her.

Having had a grumble, Kouvar Korro would feel better and would return home, where she would do her housework cheerfully.

Their single-storeyed house consisted of two rooms with earthen floors and a hall the length of the two rooms, with a hearth at the end of it, where Kouvar Korro would do her cooking; at the back was a small courtyard, of the same area as the house, with two large mulberry trees in it. In the shadow of those trees were a few hens that clucked about and a big flame-coloured cock with a red comb and a shrill crow, to which Kouvar Korro would respond with a crude but innocent exclamation every time she heard it.

Kouvar Korro had only one vice: cleanliness. Almost every other day she would rub the earthen floors of the rooms and the hall with white clay; every day, she would wipe and polish all the tinned vessels, she would dust the ceilings and the walls, she would wash with soap and water the windows and even the threshold of the front door, as well as the stone placed by the entrance to sit on. Every minute she would stroke and rub the various objects in the house. She would not only clean and polish the roasting-spits with ash after they were used, but she would do so every day. Those who entered their house would derive enormous pleasure from the cleanliness of the beds, the walls, the floors, the vessels and every single object there.

Avedis Amoudja would not attach any value to all this. When people pointed out to him that his wife looked after their home with such care that it smiled, he would reply:

'Yes, of course: she is a woman, isn't she?'

And it would happen that, in spite of not going home for lunch, Avedis Amoudja would return in the evening with something wrapped up in his red handkerchief, which he would hand to Kouvar Korro silently. What he had brought would be, without fail, something which she was very fond of. Upon taking the handkerchief from his hands, Kouvar Korro would forget everything: she would bend down, take off his shoes for him and give him his loose, indoor ones to wear. These would be a pair of old shoes, weighty with patches, but stretched out, so that he could slip his feet in and out of them with ease. When Kouvar Korro squatted to take off his outdoor shoes for him, Avedis Amoudja's manliness would be profoundly gratified; having calmed down and with his soul soothed, he would smile at her and, indicating what he had brought in his handkerchief, he would say tenderly:

'I have brought it for you.'

Kouvar Korro would go mad with delight, she would stand in front of him and exclaim:

'My sweet little bird!'

The man whom she called her 'sweet little bird' had a moustache that reached his ears; a pock-marked, squat, dark-purple nose; a lower lip, thick and cracked in the middle; prominent cheekbones; ears as large as mulberry leaves and covered with a thick growth of hair, which the barber would trim when he cut his hair.

But this amiability would not last long: the role of a husband as Avedis Amoudja understood it was to scold his wife constantly.

'The sparrows will not let me sleep in the morning!'

'What am I to do?'

'What are you to do? You are a wife: go and chase them away!'

'Well! Do you think I have nothing to do but frighten away sparrows?'

'So you've started wagging your tail again, eh?'

'And you've loosened up your jaws, have you, you lout?'

'Stop growling or I'll cut off your tail!'

'Aren't you ashamed of yourself to start a brawl like this every night?'

It would happen that Avedis Amoudja would grow so angry that he would not go to bed, but would lie down in one corner of the room and go to sleep without covering himself up; but Kouvar Korro would take the blanket and spread it over him, that he might not catch cold.

'The devil says, don't you cover him up, now!' would mutter Kouvar Korro, but she would do so all the same.

In the middle of the night, Avedis Amoudja would wake up and see his wife's solicitude in spite of his hurtful and unbecoming words, he would feel remorseful for what he had said, would get up, undress himself and would go and sleep with Kouvar Korro and, embracing her, he would say:

'Blood cannot turn to water.'

'Cover my back properly!'

'Are you awake?'

'How did you think I could sleep after those words?'

'I felt cold, you know,' Avedis Amoudja would change the subject.

This time Kouvar Korro, too, would embrace him and everything would be considered smoothed over.

Avedis Amoudja demanded that his wife should not answer back when he said anything to her. It would happen that she did not, and he would not pursue the argument and so no quarrel would take place.

Avedis Amoudja would always say:

'Look, wife, if I say something, don't answer back; it wouldn't kill you.'

'But why shouldn't I?'

'You are a woman!' he would conclude.

And Kouvar Korro would lament:

'I wish I had been a stray cat, instead of a woman!'

She would sometimes bring in other men as examples.

'Look at Aznavour Effendi!' she would say. 'Look at him, he is also a man, but he doesn't behave like you!'

'O-oh! What kind of a man is he?' Avedis Amoudja would retort, scoffing.

Kouvar Korro could not understand what her husband's idea of a man was: Aznavour Effendi was wealthy; he was one of the handsomest men in town; he was a wonderful horseman—whereas Avedis Amoudja would not even ride in a carriage, in case the horses bolted! Aznavour Effendi had disliked their old house, so he had a new one built; he used to keep his wife and daughters in furs; he used to send them to the country every summer for a holiday. How was it that Avedis Amoudja was a man and Aznavour Effendi was not?

And Kouvar Korro would demand an explanation.

'It shows you don't understand these things!'

'What do you mean, not understand? I understand them all right!'

'If you do, why do you ask then?'

'I want you to tell me!'

'There you go again, just like a woman!'

'You are mad, man!' Kouvar Korro would conclude.

Every now and then, it would happen that they would not quarrel; and they would both be surprised at this.

'We haven't had a quarrel today, man!' Kouvar Korro would point out.

'You are right, we haven't! How has that happened?'

'It looks as if the devil isn't out of sorts!'

'Bah, you're the devil!'

'I'm not!'

'You are!'

And they would begin quarrelling.

Whenever they happened not to quarrel, at night they would lie in bed with their breaths mingling.

When they lay thus face to face, Kouvar Korro would say happily and with tears of joy:

'Oh, why couldn't it be like this every day, man?'

'Yes, it would be good!'

'Why do you quarrel, in that case?'

'Who quarrels: you, or me?'

Seeing that an argument would start again, Kouvar Korro would remain silent, in order not to disturb the peace. Avedis Amoudja would be very pleased that his wife had not answered back and he would take her into his arms, would rub his moustache against her face and say:

'My precious soul!'

The years went by, but their four feet did not turn into six. Kouvar Korro remained unfruitful.

'Ah well, you haven't managed anything that way either!' Avedis Amoudja said to his wife one day, this time not in a tone of disdain and rebuke, but one of deep sorrow and regret.

And Kourvan Korro replied:

'What's it go to do with me? You are supposed to be the man and we've seen how much of a man you are!'

Avedis Amoudja felt as if he had been slapped on the face; as if a giant hand had picked him up and dashed him to the ground.

Kouvar Korro's words were hard.

For a whole week, there was not a single argument between them. Avedis Amoudja spoke quietly and gently; he could not sleep at night; he smoked incessantly and sighed away.

Kouvar Korro's words had deeply wounded him.

'What are you fretting for, man?' she asked one day. 'Why don't you go and see the doctor?'

Avedis Amoudja did not reply, but he called on the doctor the following day. The latter examined him for a long time and finally said:

'There is nothing wrong with you. Bring your wife and let me have a look at her.'

'What do you want to look at her for, my dear friend?'

'There must be something the matter with her.'

'Is that so?'

'That's what it looks like.'

'All right then, I'll bring her.'

Avedis Amoudja left the doctor's consulting room and, standing in the street, he muttered to himself:

'Bring your wife and let me have a look at her, eh? We have seen a lot of fellows of your sort, doctor effendi; we've cottoned on to your idea. You won't even see the edge of my wife's pants. You keep off her!'

When they advised Kouvar Korro that if she wanted to have a child she should go to the Jermouk Spa, Avedis Amoudja did not spare anything to make this possible for her.

Kouvar Korro's unfruitfulness was wrecking his manhood.

But the Jermouk Spa did not help either.

Kouvar Korro remained unfruitful; while Avedis Amoudja stubbornly refused to take her to see the doctor.

'I am not going to throw my honour into the street!' he would say.

Women who had children, however, would envy Kouvar Korro.

'You are lucky,' they would say, 'you have no children or anything; you can pull your shawl on to your head and go wherever you like! Ah...!'

But the anguish of being childless would consume Kouvar Korro; especially that they had persuaded her that if she had children, her husband would change completely; that he would treat her more tenderly and there would not be any quarrels. She would take other people's children in her arms, would give them sweets, and would embrace them firmly to her bosom. When Avedis Amoudja saw his wife fondling them thus, he would say:

'What do you want to make a fuss of other people's bastards for, my dear?'

When Kouvar Korro did not answer and looked at him pitifully, as if asking him for a child, he would add:

'What a nice little brat he is!'

'Yes, he's as sweet as a snowdrop,' she would whisper and would wipe her tearful eyes with the corner of her apron.

The years passed by, but Avedis Amoudja's and Kouvar Korro's relationship did not change: the quarrels continued, but these had become commonplace and they even joked about them. When they finished squabbling, they would begin to recall with laughter how it had all begun and how it had ended: you said so and so, and I replied so and so, and they would laugh as they assessed which one of them had replied the more sharply, which one was sat on and which one was the winner. When Kouvar Korro met her neighbours, she would say:

'I started a quarrel with my husband and got the better of him!'

Often when Avedis Amoudja returned home from the market, he would go to Kouvar Korro and, with a slight smile under his moustache, he would say in a quiet voice:

'Well now, wife, what do you say, shall I drink my rakki before I start a quarrel, or shall I start a quarrel first?'

Kouvar Korro would agree that it would be better if they quarrelled first and then he had his drink of rakki.

As for the excuse for a quarrel, that was ready, waiting.

'Has that dog been here again?'

'Ye-es!'

'I'll break his legs,' Avedis Amoudja roared at once.

'Shut up, you lout!'

'You have answered your man back again, you bitch!'

'Be ashamed of your age!'

'Shame is for women!'

'My curse on your head!'

'Stop growling now, and bring my rakki!'

Kouvar Korro would bring the rakki immediately.

And who was the 'dog' in question?

It was one of Kouvar Korro's relatives, who had bought a paraffin-can from Avedis Amoudja's shop years earlier and had not paid for it.

He had not done so with any intention of trying to avoid paying, but because, without consulting Avedis Amoudja, Kouvar Korro had told this relative that his brother-in-law would let him have the can as a present. But she did not reveal this to her husband even afterwards, nor did she ever do so until the end; and Avedis Amoudja remained under the impression that the 'dog' had walked off with the money.

Many, many years went by.

A thin layer of snow sifted down on to both their heads; the sharp points of their quarrels were blunted; very slight changes took place in the house: one of the beams across the ceiling split and collapsed; a pane of one of the windows broke and they stuck a piece of paper across it temporarily, oiling it with the kernel of a walnut—in spite of the fact that, being a tinsmith, Avedis Amoudja was also a glazier; the stone of an apricot had fallen between the two mulberry trees: it sprouted, grew, and began to give fruit.

One day, when Kouvar Korro put in front of Avedis Amoudja a bowlful of apricots, washed with the icy water from the well and picked from the very tree which had grown by itself at the back of the house, he reminded his wife once more of her own unfruitfulness:

'You couldn't even manage to do what this tree has done; you didn't give any fruit.'

He reminded her of this at a time when she was past fifty-five and nothing could have helped her to have children, like a plant dried up from the roots, which no spring, fired with green, could awaken.

Kouvar Korro replied:

'It's up to the man to do the trick, not the woman!'

Once more, sorrow descended upon Avedis Amoudja's soul like a heavy, black cloud upon earth; he pretended not to hear her and continued:

'If I had had a son, I would have got him a flute, so that he could blow it... We didn't even start one... The sharp point of God's roasting-spit got at us!'

Kouvar Korro was even more upset and said aloud, crying:

'I would have hung the alphabet-board round his neck and sent him off to school in the mornings...!'

The sorrow of being childless began to consume Avedis Amoudja more and more when he saw that other men of his age, tired of working, would either do very little work or sell up their shops and retire and with their rosary between their fingers they would go and sit along the sunny side of a wall and relate folk tales and stories of old, and when the church bell rang, they would stand up and go to evening prayers: their sons having grown up and taken the burden of the home on to their shoulders, they would say to their parents, 'You sit and rest at home and enjoy yourselves; you have worked all these years, we will do the work now and we can all eat together.'

Kouvar, in her turn, would go to the neighbours, talk to them of her unfruitfulness and cry.

'What happened, dear, that you couldn't have a brat?' the women would ask.

Kouvar Korro would reply:

'How should I know what the matter is with my worthless man?'

Avedis Amoudja had now reached the age of sixty-five: his hair had turned completely white, and he still had to go to his shop every morning, where he would bend the sheets of metal, curve them, hammer them, work the bellows and tin the finished articles, to earn a living for Kouvar Korro and himself.

Sometimes he would go to work so early, in order not to lag behind with the orders, and Kouvar Korro would say:

'It's still dark, man; you shouldn't go out, the wolves won't have run away from the town yet!'

'Oh, don't listen to such things, wife, the wolves wouldn't touch me!'

During the latter years, when Kouvar Korro saw that the income from the shop was decreasing a little, she too decided to earn some money. She spoke to Avedis Amoudja about this.

'Are you mad or something? What do you think you can do to make money?' he asked.

'I'll take carpets and wool to the stream and wash them,' she replied.

'You sit tight where you are; I have still got my strength!'
concluded Avedis Amoudja.

But Kouvar Korro did not listen to her husband: her conscience
would simply not let her rest, for the old man used to get so
very tired. Secretly from him, for a few days, she took some
carpets to the big stream that flowed along the edge of the town,
she washed them and received a little money; the second time,
she took some wool there, which she pounded for a long time,
rendering it white and soft; but the poor old woman of fifty-eight
could not stand the iciness of the stream, she caught a chill, lay
in bed for a few days, and died.

Her death had almost no effect on Avedis Amoudja, especially
since it had come about through her ignoring his words. Calmly
and without any tears, in company with a few relatives, he took
her to the cemetery, had her buried there, and returned home.
When the mourners crowded into the house, Avedis Amoudja
himself opened the cupboard, brought out the bottle of rakki,
filled the glasses with his own hands and, offering drinks to all
those present, said:

'Well, this is the way of the world: there is life, as there is
death!'

Outside, the autumn gale was whistling: yellowed and reddened
leaves floated down from the trees. By the evening, the fresh
mound of earth above Kouvar Korro's tomb was covered with
autumn leaves.

Avedis Amoudja sat at home with the other mourners, related
stories of bygone days, and drank rakki.

Those who left the house said:

'He doesn't care at all!'

A few of the women relatives stayed in Avedis Amoudja's
house, for it was the custom not to leave the widowed husband
alone for a few days. The last of these went on the eighth day after
Kouvar Korro's burial and Avedis Amoudja was left all alone.

On the first night the loneliness seemed strange, but he consoled
himself:

'Pretend that she has gone to Jermouk,' he said to himself.
drank a little more rakki than usual, lay down and went to sleep,

In the morning, for the first time in his life, Avedis Amoudja
took the broom and swept away the yellow leaves of autumn,
which the wind had brought and piled up against the back door,
making it difficult to open.

He even thought that such a thing had never happened in previous years. It did not occur to him that it had been the same every year and that Kouvar Korro had always swept them away, so that when he woke up from his sleep they had not been there for him to see.

He swept the leaves, cleared the path, went inside, drank down a few glasses of rakki and, without having any breakfast, he left the house to go to the shop.

His going without breakfast also seemed strange to him, but again he consoled himself, saying:

'Pretend that we had quarrelled together and I had gone out without breakfast.'

The neighbouring shopkeepers did not notice anything out of the ordinary about him. Avedis Amoudja greeted them in his usual way, opened his shop, went inside, put on his leather apron, lit the fire of the forge, sat down and began to fashion the sheets of metal.

Towards noon, the butcher opposite brought some newly-slaughtered mutton, hung it up and began to call:

'Hey! Hey! Hey...! What I have for sale is not mutton, but pigeon, yes, tender pigeon...!'

Avedis Amoudja raised his head: the meat was indeed fresh and fat. He stood up and, still wearing his apron, still with his spectacles perched on his nose and tied to his ears with a piece of string, he went across to the butcher's and, examining the hanging mutton with admiration, said:

'Cut me a good kilo of this!'

He took the meat back to his shop, did a little more work, then he stood up, shut the shop and, taking the meat with him, he went home.

When he thrust the key into the lock, he suddenly remembered that Kouvar Korro was not there.

He went inside, put the meat in the usual place, sat down, looked around a few times and suddenly shouted loudly:

'Kouvar, my dear...!'

There was no reply...

He shouted once more, but this time he broke down at the sound of his own voice and began to cry. Avedis Amoudja was crying for a woman with whom he had quarrelled almost every day for a little less than half a century.

'Kouvar, my dear, where have you gone to? Come back to me...!'

He seemed to want to hurt himself: he spoke aloud his inner feelings and was affected by his voice and cried.

'Kouvar, my dear, I have brought you some meat, will you cook it for me, Kouvar...?'

Because he was not in the habit of crying, he sobbed in a peculiar way and in his misery, loneliness, and advanced years he looked at the walls and said:

'Kouvar, my lamb, come back to me; where have you gone to...?'

He stood up, went into the inner room, from the lower shelf of the cupboard he brought out Kouvar Korro's shawl, which she used to wear round her waist; he pressed it to his nose and breathed in deeply and sobbed for a long time.

Then, leaving the meat where it was, he went out of the house, shut the door and made for the market once more. On the way, he bought some bread from the baker and some olives from a stall a few paces beyond, and went to his shop; there he put the bread and olives he had bought on to a clean sheet of tin and began to eat, shedding silent tears on the bread and olives.

The next-door shopkeeper, Toumadja Akhbar, called on him, but he did not notice that Avedis Amoudja was crying silently as he chewed the bread, and he said:

'Now that you are on your own, you are eating in the shop, eh?'

Avedis Amoudja wanted to say something but his lips contracted; he tried to restrain himself, but he could not and, with the half-chewed bread in his mouth, he began to cry aloud. Toumadja Akhbar was also upset: he, too, had lost his wife, two years earlier, and he joined in the weeping, but his crying was less intense, for time had dulled the acuteness of his sorrow. Avedis Amoudja put his hand into his pocket to bring out his handkerchief, but he did not have one. Crying and sobbing, he said:

'I have never been without a handkerchief before, Toumadja Akhbar; my wife used always to put one in my pocket.'

He stretched out his hand, took hold of his leather apron and wiped his nose flooded with tears; then he asked his neighbour:

'Did you use to quarrel with your wife also?'

'Ah well, it's the way of the world, it would happen from time to time!'

'I used to start something every blessed day!'

Avedis Amoudja did not speak any more, but only cried until his neighbour departed.

A week had not gone by before the house was completely transformed and became dirty: a thick layer of dust settled on every article; the white linen turned yellow, there was no one but himself to do the washing; cobwebs hung from the ceiling and the walls; he did the cooking himself, making the very simple dishes which any man could prepare; he would not wash up the dishes for days, but would only wipe them with some paper and use them again.

Kouvar Korro had left an immense void in the house and in Avedis Amoudja's soul.

The more the days went by, the more his sorrow deepened. He sought Kouvar Korro in the way a mother bird would seek her lost chick: he would wander about ceaselessly in the small space of this house, alone, and he would call out loudly:

'Kouvar, my dearest Kouvar, where have you gone to? Come back to me, come back...!'

Almost every evening he would open her chest, would bring out her clothes, stroke his face against them and cry. The crying would turn into a sorrowful lament when he recalled what he had quarrelled about on the day she had worn one or the other of the clothes.

'Come back, Kouvar dear, quarrel with me, I swear I won't say a word; come back, come back...!' would call Avedis Amoudja.

The following winter he fell ill. He had not covered himself up properly in the night and had caught a chill. There was not a soul to give him a glass of water even. He was barely able to get up and go to the cupboard, from which he took some rakki to rub on his body and warm it. Somehow he managed to apply it all over, except for his back, the part of his body which ached most of all. Avedis Amoudja felt wretched and, looking beyond into the void, he called out:

'Kouvar, come and rub my back with some rakki, I have caught a chill!'

This man, who, when people talked about Kouvar while she was still alive, used to become annoyed and ask if they had nothing else to discuss, would himself now talk about his deceased wife to every friend, relative, acquaintance, and neighbouring shopkeepers he met. He would enumerate her virtues, presenting even her failings as virtues.

'I had such a quarrel with her one day that the whole world was covered in smoke and dust!'

The very slightest incident would remind him of his departed wife.

When the cock of the house circled round one of the hens, sweeping the ground with one wing and emitting a deep, hoarse cry, Avedis Amoudja would whisper:

'See that? The cock has a mate and I haven't!'

When he put the first mulberry or the first apricot of the season into his mouth, he would recall Kouvar Korro and his tears would not let him swallow it properly.

He remembered how once, many years before, Kouvar Korro had suggested going to the photographer and having some pictures taken and how he had refused, considering it a shameful thing to do. He rummaged in the cupboard and found a photograph of her as a young girl. He took it to the photographer together with one of himself in his youth and asked him to put them together and enlarge them. When he brought this picture home, he hung it up on the wall, looked at it lengthily and said:

'You died and went away, my Kouvar, it was then that we joined together...!'

Everyone was amazed and would not believe it when the news spread that Avedis Amoudja had gone to the cemetery and had cried his heart out over Kouvar Korro's grave for a long time.

Avedis Amoudja was left all alone in the world, alone, aged and forlorn. He could not find a single item of consolation in his life; there was not a single flicker of hope or happiness to shine on the dark horizon of his old age.

One evening, as he was helping himself to some rakki, his eye fell on a small packet in the corner of the cupboard. He decided not to touch it.

'My Kouvar must have put it there, let it stay where it is,' he thought to himself and shut the cupboard door.

But before going to sleep, he thought of the packet again, got up and, with trembling hands, he took it to the lamp and opened it. When he saw the contents, he began to lament loudly:

'Oh, my Kouvar, I would sacrifice my very life for your soul! I wish my tongue had dried up and my eyes had become blind!'

Avedis Amoudja beat his knees and lamented, as if his wife had just died and her coffin were there before him.

In the packet, he had found flowers of a kind which were an excellent cure for coughs and very difficult to find. Kouvar Korro had wandered about the mountains and the valleys and had picked those flowers and dried them, so that Avedis Amoudja would drink the infusion made with them to cure his cough in the winter. The packet was the last of her attentions towards her husband.

'Bless your fingers, Kouvar, how did you find these flowers...?'

There was no one to say a few words of consolation, to move the packet away from his sight and pacify him; he was alone, and kept gazing at the desiccated flowers, breathing in their aroma and sobbing.

One morning, as Avedis Amoudja opened his shop, he noticed that Toumadja Akhbar's shop was shut. This seemed strange to him, as the other was always there before him. He waited until midday, but Toumadja Akhbar's shop did not open.

'He must be ill,' thought Avedis Amoudja.

But by the evening it became known that Toumadja Akhbar had stayed away because he was getting married that day.

'Well, what a low son of a dog!' exclaimed Avedis Amoudja when he first heard the news. 'Well, well, well! How could a man bury his wife and get married again...! What has the world come to?'

Toumadja Akhbar went to his shop two days later.

'What was I to do all alone in the house? I had started playing with my own shadow!' reasoned Toumadja Akhbar.

Avedis Amoudja shook his head doubtfully.

About that time, he met an acquaintance who, upon seeing Avedis Amoudja looking so very sad, said:

'Now, you mustn't brood so much, Avedis Amoudja; you are already old, what would you do with a wife at your age?'

Avedis Amoudja replied:

'You idiot! It is after sixty that you need a wife!'

'Really?'

'Do you know Toumadja Akhbar?'

'Yes, I do.'

'Well, he got married after sixty!'

'If that is so, you had better get married, too! A woman's a woman!' the acquaintance counselled him.

Avedis Amoudja was shaken.

'I? Marry?'

'Yes, get married!'

'Take a new wife, eh?'

'Yes!'

This advice did not please Avedis Amoudja, but when he left the other and went home, he could not forget it. A few days later, he met the same acquaintance in the street again. He stopped him and said:

'You know, you have lit a light in my head.'

The man had forgotten the episode and could not follow Avedis Amoudja's remark.

'I don't understand what you mean.'

'You told me to get married again.'

'Ah yes, and I'll repeat it again. Take yourself a new wife; a new one is even sweeter.'

'Sweeter?'

'Ye-es!'

When Avedis Amoudja asked Toumadja Akhbar:

'How is your wife?'

The other replied:

'Just like sugar!'

The idea of marrying a second time was planted in Avedis Amoudja's head. He became more lively after that. He had let his beard grow for some time; he went and had it shaved clean, and had a new pair of trousers made of woollen cloth; he began to put in an appearance in the cafés little by little and, on Sundays, in the porch of the church.

He was now frequently seen in the Lower Quarter of the town, which was altogether unusual for him, since he had neither relatives nor friends there.

In a small, dilapidated cottage in the Lower Quarter there lived all alone a widow named Takoug Doudou. Avedis Amoudja had known her husband years earlier, and she had offered him rakki on several occasions when he had visited them, during the time he lived in the same quarter.

As people said, the reason for Avedis Amoudja's loitering about the Lower Quarter was Takoug Doudou, whom he had seen coming out of church and had remembered that it was some years since her husband was no more.

After loitering about the Lower Quarter for a week or two,

one day he saw Takoug Doudou standing at the door of her dilapidated cottage, with her hands folded together resting on her abdomen, under her apron. Avedis Amoudja approached her and asked:

'How are things with you?'

'You ask how things are with me: well, not so good!' replied Takoug Doudou and sadly looked up at the sky, which was turning black with clouds laden with rain.

'It's going to rain.'

'That's what I mean.'

'Let it! What does it matter?'

'The holes in my roof are all as big as this,' replied Takoug Doudou, indicating the size of the openings in her roof.

'That's nothing! It isn't as if it was death. Something can be done about it. Let me go up and have a look,' said Avedis Amoudja and turned straight towards the ladder leading to the roof. He wore himself out for more than an hour and repaired the holes in the roof; with his feet he stamped down and strengthened the earth that covered it, and he climbed down just as the large drops of rain began to fall from the sky.

Takoug Doudou was deeply moved by this friendly gesture and would not let him go immediately; she made him sit on a chair and, opening the cupboard, offered him two glasses of rakki.

It was a long time since Avedis Amoudja had had a talk with a woman: he was delighted and wanted to stay on a little longer.

'I want to wait a little more, to see if the rain will come through,' he said and looked at the ceiling.

'Ah yes, that's good! And the rain is pelting down outside!'

And so Avedis Amoudja and Takoug Doudou sat opposite each other and had a long talk about this and that, about the past and the present.

In the end, Avedis Amoudja said:

'We-ell, Takoug Doudou, you and I are both alone in this world!'

'Oh, no...! What's this you say...?'

'Yes, my Kouvar died...!'

And Takoug Doudou saw with her own eyes how this aged man of sixty-five, this uncouth man cried like an infant, over his dead wife.

This fact made a very deep impression on Takoug Doudou and she joined him in his sorrow.

The following morning, she told all her women-neighbours about the incident and added:

'Lucky is the woman who dies before her husband, that she might not cry over him, but he over her.'

From that day, Avedis Amoudja appeared often in the Lower Quarter and especially in Takoug Doudou's cottage.

The rain had not been able to penetrate through her roof.

'I won't ever let a drop come through it again!' he had said with determination.

'May you have a long life, Avedis Amoudja!' she had replied.

After the rains, when the snow came down, he took to going and clearing it away from Takoug Doudou's roof. When the first fall of snow stopped towards morning, he went to her cottage, climbed on to the roof without telling her about it—the ladder being on the outside—and he began to clear away the snow. Takoug Doudou was still asleep and it was Avedis Amoudja's walking about on the roof which woke her up.

'Who can that be on the roof clearing away the snow?' she said to herself and went outside.

'It's me, Takoug Doudou!'

'Oh, you are taking so much trouble!'

Avedis Amoudja did not reply and with the handle of the wooden spade at his abdomen, he pushed the snow towards the street.

Takoug Doudou went inside. She no longer had any doubt about Avedis Amoudja's intentions. And having come to that conclusion, she felt profoundly happy, and was enveloped with a sense the like of which she had not experienced since her husband's death. Unable to wait patiently, she went outside again and called out in a loud voice:

'Avedis Amoudja! Avedis Amoudja...!'

He again came to the edge of the roof, where he stood and, in a demonstrative manner, wiped his sweat.

'Avedis Amoudja, when you have finished come down; I've got something to tell you!'

'All right, I'll come!'

Takoug Doudou prepared to give him breakfast.

Shortly, Avedis Amoudja appeared inside.

'Oh, thank you for taking so much trouble over me!'

'It's nothing!' he replied.

Takoug once more offered him two glasses of rakki and made an omelette for him this time.

'You shouldn't go to all this bother, Takoug Doudou.'

'It's no bother at all! For a friend like you, it is my duty to sacrifice a lamb, but I haven't got one.'

'Your word is worth a thousand lambs, Takoug Doudou,' he said with warmth.

On one of his snow-clearing days in the middle of winter, Avedis Amoudja opened out his heart before Takoug Doudou.

And in the middle of winter, Takoug Doudou sold her cottage to some people who were looking for a home, and herself moved to Avedis Amoudja's house, as his lawful wife, having been married in church with full ceremony.

As to how Avedis Amoudja brought the matter to a head, no one came to know.

A new life began for him, a spirited, gay and happy life, like daybreak after the night.

'The world is a good place to live in and I didn't know it,' he would say to everyone.

In a few days, Takoug Doudou revived the ageing home: she cleaned, rearranged, washed, ironed, and mended everything. It all began to smile as before, the pots and pans regained their former shine.

'Oh, my Takoug, I would die for your soul! Don't you tire yourself so much, I'll do it for you!'

And he would hurry to help her, not letting her lift and move even the lightest article in his presence; this was the man who had lived with another wife for a little less than half a century and had not raised a little finger to help in the house.

When those who had known of his sorrow, but were unaware of his marriage, met him, they were surprised to see him changed and they would ask:

'What's happened that you are so...?'

'Haven't you heard, I've got married?'

'Really? What's she like?'

'Oh, just like cream!'

Although noticeably bent, Avedis Amoudja was in such high spirits that he seemed to fly about.

When Takoug Doudou brought the rakki and put it before him, she would sit next to him and bid him 'good drinking': Avedis Amoudja would be in seventh heaven and he would hasten to put the soft cushion from under his arm, behind her back, that she might rest against it.

'Rest your back, my Takoug, don't tire yourself!' he would whisper.

And referring to the wool with which the cushion was stuffed, he would add:

'It was Kouvar—may God rest her soul—who fluffed out the wool for it.'

In spite of all his tenderness towards her, Takoug Doudou did not like it when Avedis Amoudja made any reference to Kouvar Korro, although she would not say anything about it herself and would make every effort to conceal her feelings. In due course, Avedis Amoudja realized this and no longer mentioned her and Kouvar Korro was altogether forgotten in that house.

One day, almost incidentally, Avedis Amoudja asked Takoug Doudou:

'Why did you stay unfruitful?'

She was unable to answer immediately, her eyes were moistened, then large tears hung from her eyelids:

'My man—may God rest his soul—had gone to Constantinople; they said he was taken ill,' she whispered finally, with profound sorrow.

Avedis Amoudja took hold of her head and said:

'You should have come straight to me...'

'One boy and one girl, no more,' she whispered.

'Ah, yes!' he exclaimed with pride.

One day, as he returned home, Avedis Amoudja heard Takoug Doudou grumbling to herself:

'Those chickens have worn me out! Shoo! Shoo! Shoo...!'

From that day he began to kill the chickens off, one by one. For fifteen days they had chicken for their meals, in order to get rid of them.

'Don't kill them, dear,' Takoug Doudou kept saying, 'the poor things!'

'Who's poor, you or the chickens? To the devil with them!' he replied.

The women-neighbours, seeing Avedis Amoudja's tender care towards his new wife and remembering Kouvar Korro, would say:

'Kouvar would have been better off without a husband, she

didn't see one happy day! Now he can't open his mouth without mentioning Takoug!'

And the days flew past happily.

Avedis Amoudja felt so young in himself that he worked ten times harder in the shop.

Takoug Doudou, who had at first hesitated considerably about selling her cottage and tying up her future with Avedis Amoudja, discovered in due course that inside this man—who was pock-marked, had a squat nose, hairy ears, a big moustache, and was physically almost grotesque—there beat the warmest of hearts.

When Takoug Doudou spread out groats or any other provisions to dry on the flat roof, Avedis Amoudja would sit for hours on the edge of the roof, smoking and guarding against sparrows descending upon them. And he would do this with pleasure, without any irritation. He would shoulder the sacks of provisions, take them up to the roof, bring them down, take them up again, without tiring or any resentment.

If it happened that Takoug Doudou filled a glass with water to drink it and, after swallowing a mouthful, paused to observe that it was tepid, Avedis Amoudja would immediately take the glass away from her and would not let her drink it.

'Wait a little, I'll go and get you some fresh water.'

'No, let me drink it, it'll do!'

'No, I'll go and get you some!'

And the old man would run tripping along to the fountain, happy and spirited, and would fetch some fresh, cold water for Takoug to drink.

'May your life be long and satisfying like this water, man!' would say Takoug Doudou, when she had drunk it down, with a final gobble.

'Bless your soul, my Takoug!' he would exclaim.

It would often happen that Avedis Amoudja would shut his shop early and run home before his usual time.

'Where're you off to like this?' would inquire the neighbouring shopkeepers.

'I want to go and see how my wife is; it's a thousand years since I last saw her,' would reply Avedis Amoudja and would hurry home.

The neighbours would laugh behind his back and say:

'He has gone really mad!'

Every time Takoug Doudou wished there were some particular

thing or other to eat, she regretted it, because it would be almost impossible to procure it at that time of the year; but it would be enough for her to express her desire to eat it, for Avedis Amoudja to find some without fail. He would leave no stone unturned until he had dug some up from somewhere for Takoug.

'Let her longing not stay inside her!' he would say.

One winter evening, when the two of them were sitting round the stove and talking, Takoug Doudou somehow happened to exclaim:

'I wish we had some stored grapes to eat!'

Avedis Amoudja did not echo her wish purposely, so that she would not try to prevent him from looking for some.

A little later, he stood up and made for the door.

'Where are you going, dear?'

'To the closet.'

'And I thought that you were...' Takoug did not finish her sentence, in case she put ideas into his head.

Avedis Amoudja went out to find some grapes. An icy wind was roaring fiercely; the telegraph wires were whistling and the tall, bare poplars leant over and straightened up again.

Avedis Amoudja headed for the Turkish quarter, because only the Turks would store up grapes for the winter. He knocked on one door; then on a second, a third, and a fourth. The fifth door answered, 'Who is it?'

'I have a sick person who is dying, and she is asking for some grapes,' begged Avedis Amoudja.

The door opened and he was given some grapes.

When he returned home, icicles were hanging from his moustache. Takoug Doudou threw her arms round his neck and, her eyes tearful with joy, she said:

'Where have you been, dear; I thought I was left all alone in the world again!'

'I went to get some stored grapes for you to eat, my Takoug,' he replied, proudly putting the bunch in front of her.

'Oh, my!' she exclaimed.

In the middle of this wintry night, in this small room of the cottage, by the dim light of a lamp, there blossomed a love deeper than that of any young couple.

When Avedis Amoudja tried to break the pieces of ice away from his moustache, Takoug Doudou did not let him, saying:

'It'll hurt your moustache, dear; wait a little until it melts.'

But he did not listen to her and broke away the ice and dried his moustache with a handkerchief and said:

'Let me see you eat those grapes, now.'

'You have some, too.'

With boundless delight, he watched Takoug put into her mouth and chew one by one the grapes which had shrunk but had become as sweet as sugar.

'Did you enjoy them, my Takoug?' he asked finally.

'Oh yes, very much!'

He went close to her, held the back of her head with one hand and with the other raised a lock of her grey hair and said:

'Now, I wouldn't change this hair with that of a girl of twenty! Eat, my Takoug, eat!'

When Takoug Doudou had finished all the grapes, as a reward for Avedis Amoudja's heroic love, cautiously looking round to see that no one heard her, she said:

'I will lie with you tonight...'

The harsh laws of nature, however, did not permit the whitened hair of those two old people to blossom anew like spring and turn black, their wrinkles to disappear, their backs to straighten, and their eyes to brighten and blink upon green meadows and fields aflame with poppies.

Takoug Doudou fell ill; she began to cough so violently that her inside seemed to fall out.

'Find a way of curing my only one, please, save her, doctor, I beg you!' pleaded Avedis Amoudja.

But there was no cure.

At the beginning of spring, when the willow had barely sprouted green shoots, Takoug Doudou closed her eyes forever.

For the last time she spoke and said to Avedis Amoudja, with her eyes, grown astonishingly bright and large, turned upon him: 'Follow me soon, man; don't stay alone in this world...!'

The turquoise sky adorned with stars crashed down upon Avedis Amoudja's white-haired head.

Once more relatives and friends gathered in the house, lifted Takoug Doudou's coffin and turned towards the old cemetery.

All the way there, Avedis Amoudja held his hand upon Takoug Doudou's forehead and wept, saying:

'Where are you going? I will be left all alone.'

People were surprised that this old man should feel such deep sorrow at the old woman's death.

When they rested the coffin on the mound of earth dug up from the grave, Avedis Amoudja bent down on to the coffin, wept loudly and said:

'My dear Takoug, give my love to Kouvar! I will also come before long, my Takoug, my spring flower...!'

The tears choked the old man and he was unable to finish his sentence.

They lowered the coffin into the grave and began to fill it with earth. Avedis Amoudja could not look any longer; he stepped back, turned his eyes to the sky, whispered something with trembling lips; then his eye caught sight of Kouvar Korro's tomb, which was some fifty paces away: he gazed and gazed, and began walking towards it. He went and knelt upon Kouvar Korro's mound of earth, a new torrent of tears flooded his eyes and his soul, and he said:

'My Takoug has also died, Kouvar. Look well after each other until I come too.'

Until then the mourners were burying an old woman with indifference, but when Avedis Amoudja went over and continued his lament upon Kouvar Korro's mound of earth, all their eyes were moistened also.

When they took Avedis Amoudja home, he continued his weeping with sorrowful lament and said:

'All I have in this world are two graves and nothing more...'!

Tell Me, Bella

THERE IS PEACE now in the Ararat Plain. Labour thrives, and turns into white cotton and golden grains of wheat. The sun rises out of the blue mountains of the motherland and, like a gigantic hyacinth pitcher, tilts its mouth and pours red wine into our hearts.

Through the lullaby of infinite peace and blossoming labour can be heard the fragmented chords of a harsh melody. The children, playing on the sun-tinted, friable soil, hear those chords and are shaken.

It is the past.

And I recall that past...

I am standing on the bridge of a ship and watching the Arctic Ocean, against whose grey waves our ship struggles, panting like a giant, and forges ahead.

The sun is so near, it swims downwards and approaches the shores of the earth: aglow like a colossal apricot in the condensed, cold air of the North, it descends to the towering icebergs and, without setting, rises again with a milky foam.

It is the daybreak of the North.

The hue of apricots is followed by the hue of lilies: twilight is immediately followed by dawn, without night. That is why flowers do not grow in the North.

In the South, the sun is small but scorching; in the North, it is big but without fire.

With pupils wide, I look straight at the sun: I appear to be seeing its fiery rocks from near.

It is cold, but my soul is warm, aflame like a rose of the South: I am enveloped in a happiness without shore, a mirth of the South. Joyfulness hangs from my soul, like resin from the date-palm.

My friends are dancing, a dance that fills the bones with ecstasy; they are dancing before the cold sun– with the warmth of the South.

We are on our way to the motherland.

We have left behind, on the other side of the ocean, big, gay cities lit up with electric stars; cities with the rhythm of steel;

cities glutted with pleasures and filled with debauchery; cities struck by torments of poverty and laden with wealth; cities with velvety lyricism; cities with golden filth; cities abundant with beams of light and tears.

War has broken out.

The whole globe thunders with battle.

The guns roar, but our ears are deaf, the cry of our rejoicing is louder than the roar of the guns.

The hour has struck for the liberation of the motherland enslaved for centuries.

We cry out with delirious shrieks, we dance in the face of death.

In all the waters of the world ships are being sunk by submarines and floating mines, but our small ship flutters about the grey waves of the storm in the North: our hearts are stormier and mightier than the rage of the enemy and the ocean.

The sun has climbed high. The crests of the icebergs are sparkling.

A hand touches my shoulder. I do not move. I look at the Northern sun, bewitched by its pure milkiness.

'We are on our way to the motherland,' whispers Setrak into my ear.

I am roused and my eyes meet a pair of bright eyes.

'It is only by looking at the map that we can tell where we are,' I say.

'We are heading directly north,' says Setrak, 'and we will continue until we are safe from the danger of submarines.'

I peer into the distance with a yearning for land.

Here are the mountains of the motherland, blue like the seas of the South.

All the birds fly away from the gardens, the fields, and the mountains, at the firing of our guns and rifles.

The ripened wheat-fields have turned golden, but remain unreaped. The horses and men grown wild trample upon the harvest of the people, while the waters of the mills flow on and the millstones turn without any grain, wearing each other away; the violet-tinted mist of the villages has vanished, for there is not a single fire-pit burning; the inhabitants have fled, terrified of the hatred on both sides; there is not the lowing of a single cow to be heard in the expansive fields. At night, the horns of the moon are inquiringly suspended above the earth.

But we fight with exhilaration.

The slaughter, the stench of blood, and the grotesqueness of the corpses, inflame our martial merriment.

Not a single grave thought alights upon our minds. The great kings and prime ministers of the world have promised to save our motherland, if we, her sons, fight vehemently.

And the blue dream lulls us, the blue of the mountains of the motherland and the seas of the South.

Not a diabolic cry of torment, terror, or carnage, disturbs our blood-stained rejoicing; even the cries of mothers, the screams of weeping, do not disquiet our demented souls.

There are children walking in distant deserts: naked, starving, terrified children. They are walking against a sand-storm; and powerless to oppose the gale, they are buried beneath the sand with suffocated screams: but peace descends upon their tormented, innocent souls.

Blood is flowing in torrents in the deserts of the South...

Lashed by the storm, struck by the sun, battered with clubs, men are walking towards death: that is their hope and their peace.

Behind the blue chain of mountains opposite, in a green field, on the leafy bank of the biblical river, there is a town buried among gardens, where roses bloom red like the blood that flows from a heart wounded with a knife; where violets pour down at night with the abundance of seas; where beside the town, on a plateau high, high above, like the turquoise gem of a ring, there is a lake embraced by its emerald shores.

That town, which is as ancient as the history written on rocks, is Setrak's native town, where his arms of infancy opened out for the first time.

It is from the roof-tops of that town that he fixed his eyes upon the smiling daisies in the turquoise of the sky. It is in that town that the fountains bubble with the coolness of diamonds.

Setrak fights on, his soul aflame with the fever of the urgency to reach that town.

It is armistice.

There is silence.

From the depths of this silence, from its innermost layers, can be heard the groans of the half-dead.

It is a silence full of anguish, a stillness wearied with lamentation, the silent wailing of a forest set on fire and turned to ashes.

It is the muted cry of skulls and myriads of bones collapsed in the sun.

The gale from distant deserts spreads out in the fields and grows still.

Let the sun tell what it witnessed with its own eyes of fire.

We dismount from the horses, Setrak and I. This is his native town.

We sit on the bank of the biblical river.

The waves come and flow past.

We stand up and walk towards the centre of the town. The windows of the houses, like blind eyes, stare into the expanse.

Setrak stops at the threshold of a house. He looks inside. From the dark and deserted depth within, his childhood flaps with white wings and calls to him. Setrak smiles. His smile flickers, like the light of a glow-worm in a dark abyss.

His childhood is calling him with the white, frothy wings of a butterfly.

We walk in the part of the town where the remnants of humans grown wild in the mountains, caves, and forests, have forgathered.

Setrak approaches them: he recognizes some.

'What news of our family?'

No one answers. Setrak awaits anxiously for a reply, but he is inwardly glad that they do not answer; they raise their heads, look at Setrak, some smile painfully and hang down their heads at once.

'At least one...one of the girls, or one of the children...?'

All is silent.

We move away from those remnants of humans; we go and sit in front of the door of a deserted house. We both gaze at the ground.

The silence grows deeper, when distant steps are heard.

I raise my head and look down the length of the sad, deserted street. A black dot appears in the distance; it seems to be approaching; it is growing nearer and increasingly faster as it advances.

It is a dog: a big, black dog. Setrak does not raise his head: his gaze is nailed to the ground. Sadness pours over him like yellow dust. The dog appears to have seen us, for it is running straight towards us, furiously, as if on the attack.

'Perhaps it is a beast enraged through eating corpses...' I think to myself, but the dog will not let my thoughts grow deeper, and I leap up terrified. At this, Setrak is roused from his thoughts and turns round. In the twinkling of an eye, everything changes. Setrak's arms open out as if to embrace someone. The dog jumps up to his chest, and man and dog clasp each other with yearning.

The dog embraces Setrak's neck with both its front paws, while Setrak holds it tightly round the back. The man kisses the animal and the animal licks the man.

'It is Bella, our family dog,' whispers Setrak, fastening his eyes on me.

No man has ever embraced and kissed his loved one with more ardent yearning than Setrak does Bella.

Bella whines, rubs her tail against Setrak, she licks and even scratches his face with her claws, she sobs like a child. At times her whine is so very human: she is saying something, she is telling a heart-rending story.

Setrak listens to her and kisses her: he understands the deepest meaning of Bella's whine, he understands every minute thread of her story.

'Where did they go, by what road?' asks Setrak, as a human would ask another human being.

Bella looks into the distance, emits an imploring cry, a mournful cry, from which, in the deserted street, the tragedy that had taken place is brought to life in all its gloom and with the flaming swords which rend that gloom.

'Bella, what happened to Youghaper?'

At the mention of Youghaper's name, Bella thrusts her head under Setrak's arms and weeps like a human.

'She says that Youghaper threw herself into the river...' says Setrak to me.

'What about Serpouhi?' Setrak asks Bella.

Bella brings out her head from under Setrak's arms, once more embraces his neck with her front paws, and lets out a tortured cry of grief. That grief seems to emanate from a human heart.

'So she, too, eh...?'

Bella seems to be saying, 'Yes'.

'Serpouhi must have died in the desert,' concludes Setrak.
'And Agopik...?'
Bella whimpers and licks Setrak's face, his hands and his clothes.
'Why didn't you save Agopik?' Setrak reprimands Bella.
'Weren't you both born in the same year?'
A deep grief descends, a grief as weighty as mortar.
'Tell me, Bella, where did you leave Mother?'
Bella looks at the sky and suddenly emits a terrifying howl.
Before our very eyes the grotesque corpse of an old, kindly
woman lies sprawled on the ground. Bella howls like the lament-
ing gale on a December night.

Grief, like a dense fog, descends from the sky and rises from the
earth.
The golden ashes of twilight sift down on to our heads, as
tangible grief.
The sun, like a stabbed heart, drains its last drops of blood and
departs to another, a happier universe...
It is night...a gigantic coffin, deep and silent...
The lid of that dark coffin is blue and nailed down with starry
nails.
The symphony of death is roaming about.
Who is it singing that silent and pitiless melody...?